Nothing for You, Love

By the same author:

DON'T CALL IT LOVE

NOUGHTS AND CROSSES

THE BELLES LETTRES OF
ALEXANDRA BONAPARTE

MANY MEN AND TALKING WIVES

Nothing for You, Love

HELEN MUIR

LONDON
VICTOR GOLLANCZ LTD
1988

First published in Great Britain 1988
by Victor Gollancz Ltd,
14 Henrietta Street, London WC2E 8QJ

British Library Cataloguing in Publication Data
Muir, Helen
    Nothing for you, love.
    I. Title
    823'.914[F]   PR6063.U32

    ISBN 0–575–03806–3

Typeset at the Spartan Press Ltd,
Lymington, Hants
and printed in Great Britain by
St Edmundsbury Press Ltd, Bury St Edmunds, Suffolk

Instead of happiness, say I,
custom's bestowed us from on high.

Alexander Pushkin
(Eugene Onegin)

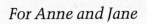

For Anne and Jane

Chapter 1

Precious little was happening in the Holloway street. The ramshackle cars were double-parked as usual. George, the Greek, who would bear false witness for anyone for a tenner, was tinkering with his old van. The door of the house was open and his father was sitting smoking on the steps. There was an air of midday loafing. It was the settled atmosphere of the Giro cheque and bits of steady work on the black market. A way of life sorted out around the system.

Eleanor Hobbs, from the dull green house with the shutters, had a train to catch. She came out with a suitcase to put in the car as some foul-mouthed drunken football youths swung in off Holloway Road and made their way down Abigail Road towards her, trying car door handles and nicking emblems and looking for trouble.

She turned away and bent into the back of the car, trying to master feelings of apprehension. 'If one of those yobs damages this car,' she was thinking, 'I'm going to kick him as hard as I can right in the testicles and then I'm going to yell for Hugo.'

But the yobs passed her, marking her presence by sending a milk bottle splintering into the next garden.

"God Almighty . . ." she said, in a loud voice, straightening up and staring after them, "For goodness' sake be careful."

Her neighbour materialised instantly with a watering can.

"Yes, clear off!" echoed Edgar Binnie, bustling tetchily as he did at work in Joy's china department in Holloway Road. "Go on, hop it, we don't want disturbances in this street." He was already neatly piling the broken glass in the gutter when the youths wheeled round and came back.

"Right, I'm going to smash you . . . asking for it, aren't you, poofy little shithead!" the biggest said, going up to the slender, daintily-dressed shop assistant and bunching his fist.

Binnie threw his arms up in front of himself. "Not on the face!"

The thug pitched into his stomach with such force that his victim's light taut body went straight over the garden wall. In a panto, Eleanor thought as she ran to help, there would have been an accompanying whistle from the orchestra pit.

Over the road, George, the Greek, stood and swore.

If swearing was enough for George, his father, a grizzled old tough from Port Said, was made of stronger stuff. He picked up the metal wing lying beside the van wheel, hastened across Abigail Road and brought it down on the back of the lout's head. It split it open.

The youths called the police.

Everybody gave their version of what had happened.

Edgar Binnie repeatedly stated he had no wish to bring a charge. Nobody but the youths wanted trouble for George's father but he'd worked himself up. He was in the mood to tackle all comers. Despite a warning, he was still arguing with the two police officers and threatening to beat them up too, when Eleanor and her husband Hugo got into their car and drove away.

Eleanor looked back as they turned out into Holloway Road. "I do wish George's father would shut up. He's going to be arrested." Even as she laughed, her legs still shook. "I'm jolly glad he and I were on the same side."

"I don't know why you didn't shout," Hugo said.

"I don't know either. So quick, I suppose. Poor little Edgar. Abigail Road is getting hellish, isn't it? It's not coming up, it's going down. I wonder what that new woman is like who moved into the end house. She'll get a shock."

"The leathery one with ankle socks and a dead white face like Marcel Marceau? I passed her making complaints about *biggutz* on the pavement outside the newsagents. I can tell you what she's like. She is humourless, plain, but exceedingly conceited. She will mismanage her children. She will pip her horn at you then race mercilessly past and into your parking space." Hugo pipped his to prevent a van pulling out in front of them. "By coming here, she's no doubt hoping to be near the heartbeat of anarchy. She's just the sort of awful cow who might attempt to discuss logic or something at the dinner table."

"Mm . . . pity." Once Eleanor would have enjoyed his description of the new neighbours but she wasn't much amused by anything these days. "Well, dog dirt is the least of her worries. She'll have mad old Mr Sharkey emptying buckets of his own urine in the gutter outside her house." She looked at her watch. "Can't you go a bit faster?" she said.

Obediently, he increased their speed but in any case they were caught in the queue of traffic. "We're in plenty of time. You've got forty minutes."

"I know but I'm not like you. I can't bear that business of diving down the platform when all the train doors are slamming. D'you know what time Ma's train arrives?" In fact, she knew exactly when her mother's train was due from Liverpool but she wanted to be quite certain Hugo knew it too since he was meeting it.

He rubbed the windscreen then he took off his glasses to rub them one-handedly on a handkerchief between his knees. His voice was distant as he peered ahead. "Her train arrives fifteen minutes after yours leaves."

"Yes, four thirty-five . . . and thank you for looking after her. She'll be gone again within twenty-four hours so it won't be a lot of trouble. You *will* look after her, won't you? Don't mention our neighbours are cracking people's heads open. She'll be in a tremendously anxious state as it is with leaving Uncle Hunt alone and the enormity of her journey to New Zealand."

"Of course I'll look after Madeleine, darling," he replied briskly. "Your mother likes me. I get on very well with elderly women. I'll take her to the Taj for the best bhuna prawn she's ever had."

"I'm only making more of this than I might," Eleanor went on, "because you said, I can't help remembering, that one of the pluses to do with me was that my mother lives two hundred miles away. Don't hurt her feelings, that's all. I mean you didn't manage to make any sort of relationship with your first mother-in-law. Of course, I know you never let her in the house."

Hugo put his glasses back on his nose, frowning quite fiercely. "There was no point in having her in the house.

There couldn't be any communication. It would have aggravated a bad situation. I wasn't going to skulk about in my own home dodging the arrows. Barbara was as sour as a lemon and Mrs Pope was like Sitting Bull."

"And you called her Mrs Pope throughout the marriage. Well, we lemons happen to mind that sort of contempt very much on behalf of our mothers."

He smiled, naughtily, almost proudly, at Eleanor's tone. "I drowve daown the M1 with yor Arnty Grace," he said, pushing his mouth out and mangling the vowels to give a ludicrous imitation of his ex-mother-in-law. "She attempted to poison me."

"Mrs Pope was terrible," his second wife agreed, hurriedly. She knew an excrutiatingly bad patch had developed towards the end of the marriage when he convinced himself that Phyllis Pope was trying to murder him.

To her dismay, Hugo relaxed their speed again and resettled himself more comfortably behind the wheel to savour the memory. "I'll never forget racing to that hospital after Christmas dinner in Morecambe with Barbara and her mother. I really believed I had about twenty minutes to live."

Eleanor semi-listened and jumpily watched the traffic. She was thinking about her own family, the other end of her journey and what she was going to find. "Where will you put the car while you're waiting for Ma?"

"I'll drop you here," he replied, when they slowed up outside the station, "while I go and park. You can get your ticket and find yourself a seat on the train. I'll follow with the cases and buy some periodicals. It's all right, Nella. There's plenty of time."

There wasn't plenty of time. She hurried up the steps and crossed Euston's dolled-up concourse to the ticket office where there were queues. She waited, shifting nervously, glancing behind her and then up at the big central clock.

"Liverpool, please."

"Single or return, love? Return's valid for three months only."

"Single," she answered quickly. "Thanks."

She glanced again at the clock then walked slowly to the platform barrier, watching all the time for Hugo.

This was the first time in all the years of going home that no one would be waiting in the car at Lime Street station to meet her. Her father was gone and the dogs were gone. Her mother's small new house would be empty and Uncle Hunt was in hospital with a leg amputated.

She walked along beside her train scanning the carriage windows to find a seat. Fridays were excluded from the other days of cheap travel so there were still plenty left. She could steer clear of all extroverts, Walkmans, toddlers and obvious rapists. She climbed on to the train and laid her long cream scarf on the seat opposite a sandy-haired mouse who was doing a crossword and eating handmade chocolates from a paper napkin. Not a figure, she calculated, to unleash his life story or kill.

By the time she jumped down on to the platform again, there were four minutes to go, no sign of Hugo, and she braced herself for catastrophe. The habitual needling was starting up in her stomach as he appeared at the barrier with her bags, and some reading for her, tucked perilously inside his arm.

The guard blew his whistle and their goodbyes were lost in the skirmish to drag her suitcases safely aboard. Eleanor leant out of the window to kiss him but the train was already moving. All she could do was to pat his arm. "Don't forget to give Bad Dog the chicken and rice. He's got diarrhoea."

Hugo nodded and half smiled. She caught that old look of silent vulnerable knowledge. She thought he knew she was thinking of not coming back.

"Give me a ring when you get there," he said.

She shouted above the noise: "I will!" And she stayed, leaning out of the window, as he waved and walked off down the platform, turned round and waved again. She went on watching him until it was no longer possible to pick out the navy jumper and the fair balding head. Hugo had a rolling, masculine walk, slightly bandy. She thought he looked back once more but the line curved, the train gathered speed and she couldn't tell.

She lifted her cases and started to reel her way along the corridor to find her seat.

Frequent rests were necessary because the train appeared endless, and she couldn't remember where the seat was. She stopped in between each carriage and stood at the open window taking deep breaths. She supposed it was the act of leaving Hugo managing on his own that made her feel breathless although it was what she wanted and, in any case, there was nothing else to be done.

She was glad he wasn't going home alone that evening to face their latest writ even though they'd always lurched along in a chaos of lawsuits and ups and downs to do with his business ventures. A moment would never come when it didn't seem unforgivable to go. Hugo was a man who'd once climbed into the bath in all his clothes when they needed washing. The worst of it was she could already hear her mother's voice.

"Well, poor old Hugo, that's what I say. You can be very

15

cruel, Nella. I used to say to Daddy, 'Is she a vixen?' And he said, 'Yes, she's a vixen.'"

But she dreaded the court cases. She felt ashamed to be seen in turmoil by the public while Hugo, as a former conjuror, seemed to thrive on them, virtually inviting writs in the first place with something heedless and cavalier about his dealings. He always represented himself and took on the judges with gusto. This time it was the local Council, who said he'd 'got up Mrs Bellfield's nose'.

They were suing for the return of the grant money. The Improvements Officer, Mrs Bellfield, had set a court action in motion against them as a last act upon her retirement.

"But I should think it's unprecedented, isn't it?" Hugo had queried over the telephone in a wondering, reasonable voice. "It must be unprecedented for a council employee to issue a vindictive writ on the point of retiring?"

Mr Wicker, Mrs Bellfield's successor, agreed that it probably was.

"As I say, Mr Hobbs," he repeated, somewhat lamely, "I believe you went right up Mrs Bellfield's nose on this one."

"I am *totally* mystified," Hugo answered.

And he probably was, Eleanor knew. He expected real life to be like his childhood existence when he'd received preferential treatment because his grandfather owned a tumbledown village in Ireland.

"I don't know how you can be totally mystified," she said, as he put the telephone down. "You harangued Mrs Bellfield about what the Council wasted money on. You went on about city wankers and transvestites and draconian Transylvanians."

"Did I?" he replied, sounding surprised and uplifted.

"Who are the draconian Transylvanians?"

"I don't remember using that expression."

16

"You did use it. You also told her that if you applied for a job telling them, 'I am a dog fucker and at weekends I meat cleave,' the Council would be so keen to support this obscure deviant, they'd say, 'Skip the interview. Start Monday.'"

Hugo tried not to laugh as he heard his remark repeated. "Well, all I can say is, it's *pretty nearly* true, isn't it. Anything monstrously outlandish helps them to overthrow the system."

"But now they're suing us."

"Let 'em." He waved his fist. "I'd like to put a horseshoe inside a boxing glove and smack that odious lantern jaw right in the puss."

Needles of anxiety sparked like fireworks in Eleanor's tummy and she was off again on one of her staccato barkings. "We must have been utterly mad to think we could ever do bed and breakfasts in this house. Why did you tell me there was nothing to it? 'A bit of muesli and toast in the morning' you said. Oh my God. Why are they suing us?"

"Mrs Bellfield was sour, inept and bovine . . . swishing down Abigail Road like the *Bismark*. She hates . . ."

"Oh Hugo, it's not just her, for heaven's sake. We're into a dispute with the architect. We're not allowed to go to Maurice Michael, that dentist, any more. Do you realise he's put 'Not to be seen again' on our cards because you disappeared twice without cancelling?"

"Thanks to Maurice Michael," he responded angrily, "I've got a mouth full of gaps like an Irish wino."

"Promise me there won't be any trouble with our new doctor. I know there will be and I'll have a breakdown. Why are we going to a private doctor?"

"If dealing with the NHS means ringing Dr Kolicassides

round the corner, and listening to Greek messages on his answerphone, it's not on, is it?"

"But that's how it is. It's what's happening. When that ENT specialist, Mr Adams-Adair, retired in Liverpool last year, his practice was taken over by a Chinaman called Mr Ho."

Hugo gave one of his yelps of laughter.

"He's brilliant, Ma says."

"And I bet Adams-Adair withheld the ultimate secret from Mr Ho."

"What secret?"

"The secret is that secretly Mr Adair's patients, those old codgers up there, will be singing a hymn of hate for people like Mr Ho. The only place they'll be wanting to see Mr Ho is working in a Chinese laundry in a Formby film."

Hugo seemed to reserve his wildest flights of rhetoric for their worst messes. "I still don't understand why we're being sued by the Council?"

"Ostensibly," he replied, "because the work on the house hasn't been completed. Their number one point seems to be the so-called gaping hole in our sitting room wall. I have told them that when the builder comes . . . when the builder comes, he will fit the fireplace in the hole . . . right?"

"I thought you told me you had to steal a fireplace from that empty council house down the road?"

"Sure. Okay, well point number two is that we have failed to put a top on the kitchen unit. According to Mrs Bellfield, who could see the top sitting there waiting, incidentally, it would not be very nice if cups dropped through into the drawers."

"I agree."

"I don't know what she means but I simply pointed out

to Mrs Bellfield that if we want a kitchen unit with no top, and cups dropping into the drawers, we are entitled to have one."

Distracted by worried thought of Hugo and the top of the kitchen unit, Eleanor actually glanced in to the right compartment at her own cream scarf, and the chocolate-eating mouse in the opposite corner, and went past. She had to come bumping back.

Her wrists were quivering with strain as she hauled her two cumbersome cases inside the carriage and up into the rack. The mouse sat tight and let her wrestle with them. She could feel sweat running down the small of her back as she straightened her clothes and sat down.

Her eyes were drawn to the pursed, closed little face curious that he had not offered help. Was that because she was bigger, because he feared she might be insulted by an assumption of female weakness or because he was nous-free? Conceivably, at a certain age it was presumptuous to imagine assistance would be forthcoming? She stilled such disquieting thoughts by pigeon-holing him as a husk who meant no harm, or good, and turned her attention to house backs through the window.

From the rows of bare oblong gardens, she tried to guess how far from London they were now. Watford probably, too early for Stafford and the dreary expanses of the Midlands. It never was a journey for scenery but getting browner and flatter and more depressing as farm animals, trees and hedges vanished from the fields. The train rocked through small stations at such speed she couldn't read the names. 'I wonder,' she said to the mouse in her mind, 'if there is a woman in the world who can see the point of you? Come to that, is there a woman over forty-four who can see the point of men at all?'

"Excuse me . . ." he spoke, half-rising then subsiding. "Er . . . the door . . . would you mind closing . . . draught in this corner?"

"Not at all," she replied, and heaved it across, sealing them together in airless intimacy. She closed her eyes. 'I want you to know, ninny,' Eleanor continued silently to the oblivious mouse, 'that by the time a woman reaches my age, there is a ball of total rage inside her.

'She no longer voices her feelings in the belief that things will change, because they won't. Men are far too busy holding forth, taking off, bossing and bungling. For the sake of self-preservation and peace, she switches off, hoping to find her own way to spiritual fulfilment in the years remaining to her. Despite what men think, this does not necessarily come via handmaidenship on a treadmill of cookery and sexual intercourse.'

That did not mean she wanted to get rid of Hugo. Only that she wanted to see less of him. It wasn't a question of leaving. She would be staying away.

To think of the future was to bring on the stomach needling. So much dread attached to it. "Let Nella see what we all come to," her father had said, when she came home, a day or two before he died. Her mother removed the clean dressing she had just put on for him and they all made optimistic comments which none of them believed.

He himself was never cast down though. He came to a state where he'd stopped golf, and the Masons, and reading in church, but he went on rereading all his favourite books with as much satisfaction as ever. The television played louder and longer and quite a bit of telephone betting went on, *sotto voce*, under the names of Mr Marmalade and Mr Scotland. But he never changed or stopped being a father figure.

On the morning he died he was at the breakfast table in the middle of reading out a letter from his sister-in-law in New Zealand, which was not addressed to him. He read in a high jaunty voice meant to sound like Pam, now an extremely fat fish in that diminutive far-off pond:

"*I think poor Lyall worries about me. I have been getting mysterious mini lapses lately when I have suddenly found myself quite unable to speak! He, and our doc of many years, dear old Roly Rankin (from Thornton Hough originally), simply don't know what to make of me* . . . better make the most of it, hadn't they?" Eleanor's father said in his own voice before continuing. "*Enclosed is a snap of Sandy with twin boys, David and Miles, aged eleven. She's a super mum, a hectically busy nutrition consultant, and a wonderful support to us. Oh, what a darling! Do you wonder we are proud of her?*"

"Oh, what a darling!" they were repeating to each other, delighted . . . and then, suddenly, that was it.

What Eleanor remembered with particular clarity was his cigarette burning on in the ash tray. His coffee was half drunk.

Her mother didn't lose her head. She was subdued but wanly businesslike as if her turn had come to be widowed and she mustn't disgrace herself. She went on adding to a list of people to be telephoned. "Ring Vera Porter, dear, will you . . . Muriel, of course, and, oh yes, Eileen's another one." While she was thinking of names, she didn't have time to think. "We must tell Mrs Bostock about Pa."

She seemed to bend physically with the weight of her sorrow and for a long time she couldn't straighten herself properly. Now, having never left the country in her life (except for skiing, her husband did not entertain the idea of foreign holidays), she was hastening to New Zealand to be with Pamela. Her brother Hunt she was leaving in Eleanor's care because the surgeon prophesied he had many good years ahead of him.

Eleanor did not believe a word of it. Uncle Hunt was a drinker. Stopping alcohol and losing a leg all at once, at seventy-five, were hardly happenings to lead to any good years. He had no wife and no projects. He didn't read and he no longer had any aptitude for social intercourse until he was tight.

But shocks are not left jagged. That was the mercy. The edges blur and the memory somehow assembles everybody together in an acceptable state. Being away made it easier. Life went on in her mind as it always had, most of the time, and she had to think twice sometimes when she was looking at photographs, to remind herself who was alive and who was dead.

In her thoughts certain images recurred all the time. Her father jumping gorse bushes was one. He was holding his stick and the dog's leash and sailing through the air, as he must have hurdled at Cambridge, looking pleased with himself and self-conscious. Showing off, of course.

In the garden, it was summer, as it always is in the memory. The passion flower was flowering abundantly above the cloakroom door. Uncle Victor, her father's friend from childhood, whizzed by with straight-backed unsmiling efficiency behind the handles of the mower. Uncle Hunt, her one real uncle, in braces and shirtsleeves, was round at the front, doing damage. Forbidden to touch plants, he raked rubbish into the wheelbarrow, tearing out lily of the valley and tiny precious poppies from under the trees. 'The bloody fool,' her father said to her mother, 'You speak to him. He's your brother.'

In the house, in a pretty apron, her mother whistled

repetitive bars of 'I'll See You Again' while she made scones for tea. Uncle Willie Crook, another of their regular weekend visitors, was calling with old copies of *The Field* and getting under her feet.

She went on rubbing flour and fat between her fingers while he lolled against the doorway to the back kitchen explaining his impromptu decision to leave for India in the morning to have a look at an interesting Lutyens' palace. Years later, Hugo would be doing the same sort of thing to Eleanor, taking off at a moment's notice, and wrecking their relationship.

The stuffiness, and the motion of the train, made her drowsy. She leant on her hand turned in towards the window in case she fell asleep dribbling with her mouth hanging open. She dozed a bit and jolted awake, then she slept properly until Crewe when she woke with a headache; something she was going to get very used to doing in the days to come.

At Lime Street station, she stood and looked about for signs for local trains. She surprised herself by not knowing how to complete the last lap of the journey. The reason was she was doing it for the first time. She'd never come home before without her father being there in the car to greet her. It gave her an abandoned feeling to go down that escalator alone and find out what she had to do. Things had changed for ever. Her one and only sheltered loving place in the world was gone. She sat down to wait for a train to take her to the other side of the river Mersey and home. A home with nobody in it.

Chapter 2

Her first shock at the hospital was hearing the nurses calling Uncle Hunt by the wrong name.

"You want Bill Quinton? Yes, love, you'll find him in the Day Room." His name was William Huntly Quinton. He'd never been called William, or Bill, in his life.

The Day Room was a vast stifling place with two televisions crackling away and old people dotted about it in attitudes of blatant non-communication. She found her uncle in a geriatric semicircle of two slumped misshapen crones and a cross-looking old man with a hat on. All were smoking. Uncle Hunt was dressed in a glaring golden Aertex shirt and a clashing emerald-green sleeveless pullover. Neither garment could have belonged to him. He was tilting forward in a wheelchair like Mr Punch on a spring, half-covered by a slipping patchwork rug and his pyjama bottom was swinging emptily where his right leg should have been. It was a spectacle of gargantuan horror.

"Uncle Hunt!"

"Mm . . . ?" His head swivelled slowly in polite response but his expression changed instantly from hazy geniality to delight when he saw who it was.

"Nella!" he said, holding out his arms for her. "Oh sweet . . . *sweet*, this is nice. I am pleased to see you." She kissed him and he held on to her so that he could kiss her again. "I've been sitting here, waiting and wondering. What a relief to see you! Did Ma get off all right?"

"Yes, absolutely fine, and Hugo's seeing her off at the airport later on."

He was grey-faced and his eyes gentle and luminous. He looked youthful, vulnerable and, at the same time, as old as old. He was not tormented though. He was tranquil.

"Well, I must say you look in fairly good form," she said. What a voice she could hear coming out of herself. "How do you feel?"

"I feel very well, thank you, Nella."

She glanced about for a chair. Could he feel well? Was he lobotomised because some blithering idiot in this hospital had stopped his drinking too abruptly? "I hope you won't mind if I join you?" She addressed the silent watching semicircle and pulled the chair up beside them. "This is my uncle. I haven't met you before because I live in London. I've come to keep him company after his operation while my mother goes to visit her sister." She spoke directly to the most alert of Uncle Hunt's companions, an elderly woman, much twisted with arthritis, with a sharp sensible face.

"Your uncle, is it? Bill told us you was coming yesterday."

Huntly Quinton threw his arm out towards her in a grand gesture. "My niece, Eleanor Hobbs, from London," he declared in a loud social voice. "And this is my very kind friend, Evelyn." It was pronounced Ever-lyn and then he stared rather vaguely at the rumpled, semi-prostrate figure in the next chair, "I don't think I know this lady's name unfortunately."

"Ada."

"What did . . . ?"

"*Ada.*"

"Ada," Eleanor said, relieved.

"Ada," echoed Uncle Hunt, with satisfaction.

"See much of Royalty, do you, in London?" Ada asked.

"No," Eleanor told her, "I'm afraid I don't. I always look forward to seeing them but we live in North London, you know. It's too far from Buckingham Palace."

Evelyn couldn't be bothered with waffle like this. "Bill and I stick together in this place," she stated in a downright Lancashire voice. "We help each other like. I mean to say, you've got to do something, haven't you. We get really depressed at times so we cheer each other up."

"He's lucky to have you looking after him." Eleanor felt he was lucky. She knew Evelyn would help to the best of her ability and she was grateful. She turned to include the old man in the hat. "You must be Mr Eastwood?"

"You know my name, madam! AFG Eastwood at your service. I expect you remember me from the Corn Exchange before the war?"

"Actually my mother told me to look out for you. She said how charming you were."

"Most kind of her. I don't believe I have had the pleasure . . . did you say she knew me?"

"She met you when she came to visit her brother."

"A gracious lady." He raised a cardboard cup of orange squash and drank.

Evelyn was nodding. "So that's his sister, is it, love, who comes to see Bill? I thought it were. I said to Ada, you can see the likeness. She's a lovely person." Her plain flat words were bluntly delivered almost as if she expected them to be challenged.

27

The curious thing was, Eleanor noticed, that none of the patients did say anything to each other. They talked to her, or they stared ahead. Uncle Hunt was getting left out of it.

"Look here, I've brought some things for you." She delved into her bag. "Here are cigs. Sweets. These jellies are the ones you like, aren't they?"

"Good-o, Nella. I've been longing for the cigaros." He started to unwrap the cellophane and all the packages slid away off the patchwork blanket.

She picked them up, reminded of the routine round a baby's pram. "I'll do that for you. Are you going to have one now?"

"Thank you, sweet. Shall we go upstairs for a bit?"

"Right." Relieved to make an escape from the group, she offered cigarettes and sweets all round, grappled with the brake system on the wheelchair, and gently started to manoeuvre their way towards the door of the Day Room.

Mr Eastwood rose too, thin and dignified. "I think I'll come with you," he called, standing with his cup of orange. His dressing gown and pyjamas were flying open at the front, "If you're going now, I'd like a lift to the West End."

" . . . not going at the moment, I'm afraid, Mr Eastwood. We're only going upstairs."

Huntly Quinton glared at him. "Stupid old fool," he said.

"Well, which way, Uncle Hunt?"

"We'll go upstairs." He sounded determined but vague.

"I'll just ask the nurses for directions." She put the brake on carefully and crossed to the reception desk to find out what he meant.

"Go along to the Yellow Room, love. There's nobody in there."

"Okay, I've got it," she said to him, swinging his chair round. "If we go down this corridor to the right, we'll find a peaceful place to talk."

"Whizzo, Nella."

'Dear God,' she was repeating silently to herself, focusing on the back of his head. Even his hair was different. It was floating and wispy and suddenly seemed startlingly white. He looked so defenceless in the green pullover and the common Aertex shirt. That's what was heart-rending. He'd lost control of his life.

So they sat in the Yellow Room and had jellies and cigarettes. He wet the tips. Eleanor had not smoked for a long time but she had to have another then another. She could have stuffed the entire packet into her mouth.

"I haven't brought Bad Dog with me this time."

"I'm sorry to hear that. He's a nice doggie." People invariably said 'doggie', she'd noticed, when they weren't interested in dogs. Uncle Hunt wasn't.

It was she mostly who raised the topics and he responded in an uncharacteristically benign and passive fashion. A few words disposed of each subject, after which they fell into silence again.

They were in a lull, smiling, when he said, "Well, I've really landed myself in something this time. I think I've had my chips, sweet, haven't I?"

"No," Eleanor replied emphatically, "you most certainly haven't. You've had a great upheaval, that's all, but you're making excellent progress the doctor says."

Each time he shifted in his chair, her heart turned over for him. She knew he was in pain and could not get comfortable. She fiddled with the pillow at his back to lodge it into exactly the right position but he was perched like a popinjay and looked as if he could topple forward at any moment.

29

"Ma said Mrs Lamb came to see you?" Winifred Lamb was the widow of his oldest friend, Matt, who had died a year ago.

"Mm . . . what's that, sweet?"

"Mrs Lamb came?"

"Very nice of her. She's a weird being, you know, but I felt she lined up differently with me the other day. I'd always thought she regarded me as a bit of a wildcat and not to be dealt with."

Eleanor laughed. She knew why that was. Her mother had described what happened when Winifred Lamb motored over to see Huntly after her husband's death, with an invitation to go and stay with her in Llandudno and some of Matt's clothes for him to try.

He was most appreciative but tight. "God bless you, Win," he said expansively, several times, as she helped him on with the garments then he sank to the floor, taking her with him. The invitation to Llandudno was not renewed.

"'Tis a great pity you didn't see Winifred Lamb as a matrimonial plum, isn't it."

"Ooh, no, not her." He pulled a face. "Win Lamb must have been hidden behind the door when God was dispensing the good looks. I suppose there's always a possibility that some extremely ancient fellow with a colostomy might be interested in her."

As their eyes met, she might have been five again, or ten, or fifteen. "Applee pee!" said Uncle Hunt, squashing his mouth out, "Mmmmmoof . . ."

Eleanor tucked the patchwork blanket into place and lit another cigarette for him. Everybody has turns in life, she'd always assumed. The first half of Hunt's life was so golden and successful that the second half was almost bound to be a sort of melancholy hell. His leg wouldn't have been amputated if the doctor had recognised there was a clot in the first place. Instead, the doctor bungled. He diagnosed 'irritation' and by the time the clot was discovered, it was too late.

"Well, Nella, I think I'll be off now." Uncle Hunt's hands were already trying unsuccessfully to move the wheels of his chair.

"Oh yes. Yes, of course." What did he want? She jumped up, ashamed that she'd exhausted him and took up her position to push. "Let's get back. Let me know if you want to stop for anything . . . the lavatory or anything?"

"No, can you take me to the bedroom? I need a handkerchief from my drawer."

She found Dawson Ward, Uncle Hunt's small room of seven beds. There was a loud scene going on involving Mr Eastwood, who still had his hat on, and a resolute little nurse with plump legs and a soft coaxing voice.

"Would you like to lie on the bed, Arthur?"

"No."

"Ah . . . come on. We're friends, aren't we?"

"We are not friends."

"I thought we were."

"Get away from me, woman!"

"The doctor wants to see you."

"Woman, take your hands off me or I shall call the police."

Uncle Hunt swivelled slowly round. "Shut your trap, you stupid old bugger!" he said.

Eleanor and he were just leaving the room when the Sister arrived, accompanied by another little nurse.

Huntly Quinton bowed to them as they stood back for his chair to pass. "Stop a minute, would you, sweet," he commanded in a rather carrying social voice, "I want a word with these ladies.

"Ladies! This is my niece, Eleanor Hobbs, who will shortly be leaving for London. I'd like dinner at once please and then I shall go straight to bed."

The Sister patted his shoulder. "All right, Bill?"

"Thank you so much." Uncle Hunt smiled remotely, still using the carrying voice. "I've decided to quit this place on Saturday," he added, as they were manoeuvring their way back to the Day Room. "I'll settle up and Bob's your uncle!"

Leaving the hospital herself, dazed with shock, Eleanor got back into her mother's car and drove at least six miles before she realised she was travelling out to Chester in the wrong direction. When it dawned on her, she turned round, and the next thing she was lost again all over Burton and Neston, districts she'd known all her life. Her mind was wandering and she couldn't pull herself together.

He *had* had his chips. Another person in the same state might not have done, might have learnt to walk again, but for him she knew it was the end, and such an end. He hadn't any friends now. He hadn't anything. And once upon a time, everybody wanted to be with him.

As a child, Eleanor had worshipped him.

"Guess who's here?" Her first proper memory was in the night with her mother whispering in her hiding-Christmas-presents voice and peeping round the nursery door to see if she was awake. "Who do you think is standing beside me? Three guesses!"

"It's Uncle Hunt!" she'd shouted, jumping up and down on the bed, because her mother's Christmas voice meant somebody terrifically exciting and a visit from Uncle

32

Hunt was the greatest excitement she could think of in the world.

Occasionally, since then, something had reminded her of his stupendous snores in the night and the special bedroom smell he created which was mingled ever after in her memory with the thrill of having him staying with them. It was a mixture of tobacco and Pears soap, laundered shirts and leather. An old-fashioned masculine smell with a lingering whiff of spirits on the air in his room.

He'd usually stayed on, long after her father started pulling faces and saying 'When's he going?'

Eleanor's only memory of the war was the air raid shelter in the dining room. She couldn't remember being in it although Liverpool and Birkenhead were devastated by bombs. She couldn't remember Uncle Hunt in uniform either but those night-time arrivals must have meant he'd come home on leave from the Air Force. With no parents living, home was with his sister. After the war, he took a job in South America because the cotton trade, once the biggest industry of the country, died out in Liverpool. Her grandfather had lost his money and died of a heart attack on the steps of the Cotton Exchange before she was born. Hunt had already followed him into cotton so that was all he knew.

By the time he started coming back on leave from Peru, which he did for three months every three years, he'd acquired a striking aura of substance and success. He brought crocodile bags and llama blankets and Eleanor's mother basked locally in the glory of having such an adventurous, glamorous brother.

The whole village took an interest in his progress, noted his dashing friends and their rapid long-nosed cars. Even the shopkeepers went on asking after Mr Hunt, as some of them still called him. Stories of his past wildness, and the houses from which he was banned when he was young, only added to his reputation.

People still laughed about him climbing up in the hall at Odd Acre and putting a chiffon scarf and bowler on Mrs Weaver's stag's head. They talked of the time he jumped on all the teapots at the golf club and the musical evening when he played the 'Merry Peasant' then poured his drink into the grand piano. One or two of them could actually remember a small boy coming on to the Parish Hall stage as Simple Simon, and pulling a dippy face for the audience. When he realised the effect he'd made, he stayed there, with his eyes sliding and his tongue lolling, getting loopier and loopier. The place was in an uproar. So nobody liked to see a handsome, amusing man like Hunt Quinton going to waste.

Eleanor's mother was not sure whether she wanted her brother to be married or not. In public, she said she did.

Privately, she was more possessive. "Poor Molly Irving is after him, hard as she can go, make no mistake about it," she'd be saying. Or "I saw that made-up doll, Dora Lacey, glinting at him last night at the Youngs. She's got terrible dyed blonde hair, gone like straw, and she's man mad. He can't see it, of course. Her name is mud in this district." And Eleanor's mother wagged her head from side to side, making a high simpering 'heh heh' sound, in the manner, she imagined, of the older nymphomaniac desperately displaying her charms. But Hunt was everybody's favourite wherever he went. And he went everywhere.

From a child's point of view, the generosity and good looks can't have amounted to much. What Eleanor enjoyed were fast bouncing piggy backs and the ecstatic hiding ghost games, with roaring chases in the dark, when something always got smashed. Best of all was the fact that he was funny. He was conspiratorial. He said shocking naughty things about bigboy and bogies which were right on her level and they laughed and laughed together. He'd a loud rollicking gleeful laugh which made other people laugh with him. He made her father seem like an old stick.

Fairly swiftly during each visit, her parents began to issue warnings to each other. "Don't get any drink out before supper, whatever you do."

"Good Lord, no. We had enough of that last night. Did you see what he poured himself?"

As a child, of course, Eleanor never noticed the drinking, although that was what wrecked Hunt's life. When his leg was amputated, the hospital went on supplying him with real drinks at first, then it was tablets and then it was nothing.

"You see, he's absolutely nothing left in life," she said to Hugo, when she rang him that evening after her visit, "I'm afraid he's just going to turn into a zombie. He can't read now or watch television. Uncle Hunt talks as if he's in a hotel but I wonder if he knows exactly what's happening to him and simply can't face it. He said he thought he'd had his chips."

"How terrible. Poor Hunt. He's had some duff cards, hasn't he?"

"Did Ma get off all right?"

"Fine." 'Sugarfoot Stomp' was playing in the background. Hugo had a huge seventy-eight collection from the days of King Oliver and Jelly Roll Morton. He sent to the States for rare records and he had occasional finds in the throw-outs at the PDSA shop up the road.

"Thank you for managing. I bet she was nervous about her flight?"

"She was nervous. I must admit she came off that Liverpool train looking unusually outlandish. She was wearing some sort of hairnet thing I'd never seen her in before and she came down the platform eating a florentine. She tried to get me to eat one which of course I couldn't dream of. Anyway, while we were bending over, messing about with the paper bag and her luggage, a really elegant guy came charging down the platform. His umbrella tip got caught in that hairnet."

"Oh, my goodness, poor Ma. Was she all right?"

"They were helpless."

Eleanor laughed too. "How's Bad Dog?"

"He's fine."

She wanted to ask if the dog missed her but it didn't seem very tactful. "What did you and Ma talk about?"

"The usual. She wants me to sell the wine cooler for her. I told her things were a bit difficult at the moment, no stuff about, and I've got that guy coming for the antiques fair from the Baltimore Museum. D'you know what she said?" he demanded, incredulously. "She said, 'How about going along looking very charming?'"

"I hope you didn't mention the writ?"

"I didn't mention the writ as it happens although I might easily have done."

Because she wasn't there, she felt a miraculous detachment from it all. It was such a relief not to be feeling knotted with resentment and so restful to be somewhere without a hole in the wall where she could answer the front door bell without bracing herself for trouble.

"The telephone went dead this morning," Hugo went on. "Jesus, you can imagine it, can't you? I gasped at the air like a landed fish then I raced outside to the telephone box. When I got back they were working on the road outside. I was so relieved I entered into a long and jocular conversation with the workmen. Pathetic, isn't it!"

Eleanor felt a wave of sympathetic giddiness. She could imagine only too well. "I suppose that builder hasn't been yet?"

"I saw Dave at lunchtime when I went to get a pie . . . drinking himself into a stupor on my money and all those Giro cheques from the DHSS. The pubs are stuffed with stupid, slow, devious builders telling each other long-winded, semi-dramatic apocryphal tales as true. To see that lazy sot, with his poof's bonnet hairdo and bundles of ill-gotten tenners spilling out of his pockets, is to really long to wring his fat neck. He promised me faithfully he'd be round this afternoon."

She sighed. "And no sign?"

"What do you think? Not a murmur. A Mr Majid called from the Council."

"Oh God. We've had it then."

"We got on very well. I gave him coffee and made him extremely welcome then I showed him the work on the house. I handled him perfectly. He was beaming from ear to ear."

"Wonderful."

"Yes. He's a lot easier to deal with than Mrs Bellfield. She was a sort of north London Doberman but Mr Majid seems to have some awareness of our problems. He could see I'd worked like a beaver. Quite honestly," Hugo said, "I got the impression he was surprised to find me so affable."

"I'm sure he was. I expect he was waiting to be harangued about wankers and transvestites."

He gave a small stifled laugh. "Why the hell should I be affable? I told him his colleague had stung like a wasp then left the Council. I must admit Majid appeared to be doing his best to be pleasant. He said how reassuring it was to find someone who still smoked, in the prevailing atmosphere. He'd come without his own cigarettes so naturally he smoked all mine."

"Well, what about the writ?"

"I've got the hearing postponed. I'll be making a counter claim in any case."

"Hugo, we mustn't get to court."

"I'm going to get in that court and really let 'em have it. All their council swindles will be exposed. I'd like to take a broad sword in with me and say to them: 'Now you're going to pay the supreme penalty!'"

A slight throb started up behind her eye. "But what happened with Mr Majid?"

"Unfortunately, Bad Dog pecked him on the arm as he stepped into our bedroom. That caused a mild hiatus but after that we established some sort of rapport. He stayed for ages talking about what bad news builders are, house prices and so forth. He told me all about a brothel for three thousand in Bombay. I tell you, once these people find a topic for conversation, they're happy as lambs. What they like is to expand into areas where they can inform you. You see if Mr Majid had been talking to another Indian, the other chap would have been arguing. They love ticking each other off."

"He recommended the brothel to you, did he?"

Hugo laughed. "Only to view, you understand. He did ask me if I minded if he made a personal remark and when I said no, he said, 'Mr Hobbs, you are reminding me pretty devilishly of a certain celebrated movie actor. His name is Michael Caine.'"

"What a joke. So what did you say?"

"I said it wasn't the first time that had been said to me

and, oddly enough, I was about to say exactly the same thing to him."

"You didn't! Is he black? Wasn't he astounded?"

"Smiling like a badger."

"But did he look like Michael Caine?"

"Mmm . . . he did a bit."

"Surely, if you've made friends, they'll stop the legal action?"

"We'll see, won't we."

They chatted for a few more minutes. Hugo was drinking coffee at the other end and yawning.

"It looks like a long job then with Hunt?" he queried. "Your mother's going to be away for at least three months, I gather?"

"Yes . . . um . . . I'm afraid it will be quite long. I can't help it. I have to stay here for him because he hasn't got anybody else. But we can come and go, you know, whenever we feel like it."

There was a silence. She knew he was thunderstruck.

"I didn't realise you intended to be there for the entire period." If Hugo had ever said 'I love you' or 'Go to hell', it would have made a difference, but he didn't. He never had. He'd always been absent on one of his needless foreign trips or too involved with the mainly self-induced trials of life. Everything was turned into a matter related to his convenience. He had no difficulty expressing himself about that.

"Of course, all this is happening at the very worst time from my point of view," he continued, with predictable irritation. "I've got several crucial things coming up. I don't see why you're . . ."

"Because he's going to die, that's why. In any case, I'm looking after the cat."

She thought she heard Hugo give one of his rude exaggerated intakes of breath. He told her he was off to France for a few days to see Monsieur Flash and his speciality magic act with light bulbs. He hoped to sell him an idea for an escape trunk he'd invented and also look into the possibility of doing a deal on some furniture. Eleanor put the telephone down feeling guilty and dissatisfied.

Being so civilised was not satisfactory. But, without passion, it was surely the only dignified way to behave? All kinds of things could be said if people were going to bed as the climax. But they couldn't be said, if they weren't. Nonetheless, she wished Hugo had said *something* although logically she didn't quite know what. Being beyond words in a relationship was all right when it was a question of twin souls not needing speech. When it was a question of apathy, it was obviously the end.

She woke up next morning with a headache. It was an unusually disagreeable sensation to be nagged awake by a pain already throbbing over one eye. Her anxiety was invading her sleep. As she dressed, she felt waves of apprehension at the thought of confronting that geriatric ward again with Uncle Hunt, perched in his wheelchair, like a nodding puppet. And she was worrying about Bad Dog while Hugo was away. It would be the first time their help, Mrs Turner, had stayed in the house to look after him.

Holding some baggy yellow trousers across herself, she went into her mother's bedroom, which had windows on three sides, to look for aspirin.

Dressing in this new glass box of a house was not without hazard. There were houses in front and houses behind, in three slightly differing designs, and their huge windows looked right in to their neighbours' huge windows.

She watched Mungo, her mother's marmalade cat, plop over the fence into the next garden and start washing in the middle of the grass. She called to him to shift himself. He stared brazenly towards the house then he dived his head into his tummy, contorted himself into a shape like bagpipes and carried on with the wash.

He'd taken more happily to this house than Eleanor had. She hated it. It was characterless but it had its own weird desolating features. In the kitchen, for instance, there was a sort of thin Formica ironing board which let down from the door of the brush cupboard. This was a 'breakfast bar', specially designed by the previous owner. Her mother had dispensed with the two exceptionally high stools which went with it and simply used the surface as a convenient place to put cooling cakes and pile up dirty dishes.

Everybody wanted boxes like it with small gardens these days, her mother insisted. Nobody wanted anything remotely old. They were lucky to get out of their other house before the windows fell out, she kept on saying. All the sills were rotten. Rowan Wood was no more than four miles away but Eleanor knew she was not going anywhere near it. The new people had already started cutting the trees down.

When she arrived at the hospital, Mr Eastwood was the only one in the ward. He was sitting beside his bed with his hat on, doing nothing. His head was hanging. Two yellow teeth were protruding from the white old face and a strand of greenish slime trailed across his chin. He had paused for reflection in the middle of something. He was naked.

"Hello, Mr Eastwood."

He didn't recognise her. "Nurse?"

"Bill's in the Day Room, love" a nurse said, passing her.

Well her mother seemed convinced Hunt was perfectly happy to be called Bill. "He says he prefers it now," she'd told Eleanor. "In fact he wishes he'd used William all along."

Having a leg off was blow enough. Having a leg cut off, and being called by the wrong name on top of it, seemed to her provocation beyond anybody's wildest dreams. Eleanor breathed deeply to prepare herself for shocks and walked into the Day Room.

She spotted him at once this time because she turned towards the same corner. He was being wheeled in beside Evelyn by the plump nurse with the soft coaxing voice. He was looking washed and fresh and wearing a navy cardigan she'd made for him. She could see his white Aertex underpants and bandaged thigh — 'stump' the nurses called it — with a tube dangling. Her uncle was gazing at the little nurse as she arranged his rug and lodged the pillow for him. "Oi oi!" he said, "You're a nice nurse. What's your name?"

"I'm Nurse Blackett."

"No, what's your Christian name?"

"It's Karen but you have to call me Nurse when I'm on duty."

"All right, Karen."

As Eleanor hovered then moved over to greet Evelyn, a be-whiskered old lady padded purposefully towards Huntly Quinton and gave him two squelching kisses. "I always do this. He's the image of my late husband, you see," she explained, beaming round with swimming post-cataract operation eyes. "He was called Bill too."

"How now, sweet!" Uncle Hunt said, "I am glad to see you. The trouble is that cakey cow will keep on kissing me. It doesn't do me any good at all."

42

"All right, Bill?" The little nurse smiled and took his hand, "I'll leave you then."

"Thank you, Karen."

"You look well today," Eleanor told him. He looked gaunt and hooked like a head on a coin. "The nurses here are excellent, aren't they."

"Beautiful kids," he agreed. "Yes, I think I'm gravitating towards this place. It could be the coming area after London and South America. Funnily enough, I haven't felt happier for a long time."

"I must say you do seem content." She breathed deeply, smelling sick.

"I am, Nella. Very content."

This peaceful humour he was in was something she had never known. His past air of brooding grievance with his lot was gone. All his life he'd incommoded people with his behaviour. It was as if he was atoning, in his suffering, by unrancorous acceptance of what had finally happened to him.

She produced the cigarettes and the peppermint creams she had brought and passed them round to those nearest to them. Old men and old women, without legs perhaps or sight or hearing. They sat along the wall, turned in upon themselves, to brood upon the past. But they scoffed the mints, and made jokes for her and boasted about their children. They were still game. There was one special one called Frank who was blind. He'd lost both legs but he chattered away, this sightless trunk, and, if there was nobody for him to talk to, he listened hard to everything happening around him. When his wife came in to see him, they sang a song together.

"D'you work in London, love?" Evelyn asked. She didn't bother with small talk. She wanted to know.

43

"I'm a guide," Eleanor told her, "I take people on walks round various parts of London."

"Ada said you was probably a teacher but I guessed you'd be on the sporty side with those long legs and being well-built and that."

"Evelyn! Only little walks." She laughed and pulled a horrified face. *Sporty*. Oh God. In her present mood she felt well on the way to middle-aged dykedom as it was. "They only last two hours, you know. We stop all the time and I have to do a lot of talking. My three specialities are a Dickens walk, a Dr Johnson walk and a tour of city churches. I'm absolutely sick of them all. It's marvellous to be having a rest."

She sat down beside her uncle who was looking neglected and shifting painfully in his seat. His bit of sawn-off thigh seemed to bob about with a life of its own. She wished she could take his hand as naturally as that little nurse had done, but there was nose-blow on it and she wasn't able to.

"People in the village this morning were asking after you," she said to him, making something up for conversation. "Several people sent their love."

"That's extremely kind of them."

"I wonder if you'll have any other visitors this week." She wished it was more likely that there would be visitors for him but she couldn't think of anybody. "Of course, it's a long way for people to come."

"It is a long way," he agreed, appearing to ponder on that. "Robin White comes fairly regularly. I expect he may look in today or tomorrow."

"*Robin comes?*"

"Yes, Robin comes. Jolly decent of him."

Years had passed but the effect of hearing his name was

44

the same as ever. She forgot Uncle Hunt's mind was muddled. She forgot Robin Stewart White had probably never been near the hospital. It was like being winded. A minute later, on her guard, she could ask casually for news of him.

"Oh, he's just the same, you know," her uncle said vaguely, accepting another peppermint. "He's a good egg."

Eleanor felt certain he was exactly the same unchanging good egg and she didn't want to see him again. Why was Uncle Hunt mentioning him now? Didn't he remember what had happened? Was it because he felt regret?

"Hugo sends his love too," she said.

"How is Hugo?" Uncle Hunt enquired benevolently. "I often think about him. Robin was asking after Hugo the other day."

Chapter 3

Robin Stewart White was a dark horse, Eleanor's mother said. What Eleanor had thought was that one discovered things gradually about Robin. When they first met him, people had the feeling they were being incredibly interesting and witty with this quietly pleasant man. They felt they were sparkling on the highest plane of civilised talk and his brief, acute responses were just what was wanted to keep them sparkling. Only later did they grasp that it was he who was the sparkler. When he left the room, the sparkle went out of it.

He was tall, a bit too bony, with assessing blue eyes. His hair was prematurely white, and a piece of it flopped continually on to his forehead. Bewitched by the silences and the penetrating stare, all women at once assumed they were needed by him. They were and they weren't. He was that rare plum in the north of England, an old Etonian, which girls rather enjoyed and their mothers enjoyed even more. Most boys locally were sent to Marlborough or Shrewsbury, Rugby or Stowe.

The Stewart Whites' family firm had a branch in Peru and Robin met Huntly Quinton in a Lima night club. On the face of it, they had little in common except their Britishness, a scattering of acquaintances and the fact that Robin's father also had an office in Liverpool.

In that atmosphere, it was enough to start with. They joined up that night in the night club and, as time wore on, their party grew more drunken. Finally, rowdily, they called for the Manager and made the disclosure that Hunt used to be Paul Whiteman's drummer. He would be happy, he said, to sit in with the band for a couple of numbers.

There was an announcement, a eulogy of the legendary American band leader and some words about the great good luck of those present in having such a distinguished musician in their midst. To delighted applause, Huntly Quinton, who had only played the drums at school, bowed his way over to the band and seated himself in front of the drum kit, making some odd little humming whoops with his mouth closed.

"¿Qué le apetece?" enquired the deferential band leader. "'Sweet Georgia Brown' . . . 'Sweet Sue'?"

Hunt chose 'Sweet Sue'. "Muchas gracias. Whizzo . . . 'Sweet Sue'. ¡Empezamos!" he shouted and started bashing.

"¡Por Dios y la Reina!" muttered the appalled band leader, realising there was some mistake. "¡Madre Mía!"

It was Robin Stewart White who extricated Hunt, smoothed things over and got him home to bed. Next time he was in Liverpool, he looked up Quinton's sister as he had promised he would.

He was invited to dinner. "He has a gorgeous deep voice," Eleanor's mother informed the family, "I've lost my heart already. How nice of him to ring us but I expect Hunt's been useful to him out there."

"Oh hell, no," her father groaned. "We don't want him. Do we have to?"

"I had to ask him, dear. What else could I do?"

"How old?" demanded Eleanor.

"I can't tell you. Older than you."

Although she was anxious to impress him, Eleanor didn't fall for Robin straight off because he was so much older. At thirty-two, he was slightly closer to her mother's age than her own and that made him somewhat remote. Sitting with her parents she felt youthful and unworldly. She desperately wanted to be noticed and acknowledged and not to fall over the furniture when his assessing blue eye was upon her. Dulcet as she might seem, she was used to attention. She enjoyed conquests. But the innocent mixture of good girl/bad girl, which proved potent enough with men nearer to her own age, was hardly likely to make much impression on a sophisticated figure like Stewart White.

He, though immensely polite, had an air of circumspection. It was as if, Eleanor decided, he was staying in first gear as far as they were concerned, but if the right button happened to be pressed, he could slip into top. No such thing happened. They ground along at the lowest level of discourse. She could still relive the embarrassments of that evening.

Her father, a reserved, reclusive man, both nervous and intolerant, could be alarmingly cryptic with guests. What he said was often unfathomable but, once underway on a subject, he seemed unable to come away from it. If he wanted to be genial, he tended to talk dogs. He could stay on dogs throughout a cocktail party.

That night, after hearing Stewart White's amusing account of his brother-in-law's drumming, he kept the conversation going at dinner with a shyly smiling description of a small role he'd taken himself to help out the drama section of the local Townswomen's Guild—on the boards he suddenly called it.

"What fun," Robin said, fixing him with a winningly attentive stare, "I'd no idea you were a family of performers."

Oh my God, Eleanor was thinking, as she jumped up and down to carry dishes. Why was Pa doing it? Why didn't he stop? She'd never heard him saying 'on the boards' before and talking in an actor's manner of wigs and rehearsals and the difficulties of tackling the all-women play. Why was he pausing and smiling and behaving in such an extraordinary way like some old ham divulging the secrets of the stage? He was covered in dog hair.

"Yes, I came to their rescue on that occasion," he continued, massaging his chin, in the new style of portentous recall, "We did *In The Mood For Murder* for the Northern Amateur Festival . . . two performances at the Parish Hall. We played to pretty . . . nearly full houses on both nights, you know. Not bad, was it? There's only one male part in the play, of course. The Townswomen hadn't got a man to do it so they were stymied."

Robin Stewart White was nodding. Eleanor's father nodded too and smiled at him. He wasn't normally given to open-mouthed smiling. "I think I acquitted myself quite well . . . what!" With a bit of a flourish, he packed some food on to his fork in the air as those, Eleanor's mother said, who didn't know any better, did in the Kardomah.

"Those dames seemed to think I managed a convincing Mr Burslam," he resumed. "He's the solicitor who arrives in . . . er . . . what might be called the time-honoured manner, to read out the will after the murder. The *Advertiser* maintained I looked the part!" They all laughed. He was big and weatherbeaten and rumpled. He looked as if he could clear a gorse bush. He looked, Eleanor thought hopelessly, more like the dog's bed.

"I don't know the play," Stewart White admitted in an interested voice. "Who wrote it?"

"Let me see . . . her name just escapes me. Some woman locally." Eleanor's father put down his knife and fork and appealed to his wife, "Can you remember, dear? A Miss Something or Other?"

Her slow maternal smile round the table said many things. "Miss Armitage," she said. "More peas, Robin?"

"That's it. Arm-it-age." He spun the syllables out as if Robin might wish to write it down, "Of course, she's no Edgar Wallace, you know, nor anything like it. It's not a bad little play though. Our group came second in the festival adjudication."

"They did very well," Eleanor's mother said, in a final voice.

"A promising career obviously lay ahead on the professional stage," Robin suggested.

"Oh . . . noo . . ." He hesitated dreamily, forming his fingers into a steeple, "Noo. I don't think theatrical digs would be quite my _métier_!"

For those at the table, there seemed no possible likelihood of ever coming away from this subject until suddenly Eleanor's father mispronounced the word buccaneer, sounding the 'bu' as in bugle, and there was an awkward silence.

In the silence, which was filled with noises of chewing and swallowing, he brought a morsel of meat out of his mouth and tossed it to the dog. Coyly ducking his head, he went on gazing at the animal while the others gazed at him. He spoke at last, in a most amazing accent. "He did well, did Dad Boling!" he said and looked up again with a loud sheepish laugh.

Stewart White could not know these were the words of an old Yorkshire nanny, now a family catchphrase. He simply assumed the dog's name was Dad Boling and that he'd done something well.

"Well done, Boling," he echoed agreeably, twisting in his seat to have a look at the black Labrador.

Eleanor's father gave him an amused, appreciative glance. "If only they could talk!"

Cripes, thought Eleanor, and jumped straight in before the dogscape unfolded any further.

"Uncle Hunt says he's going to send me the fare to Peru for my next birthday."

Getting a turn of the winning stare was heady stuff, she discovered, as Robin Stewart White's penetrating blue eyes searched hers and seemed to see into her soul.

"And you're going, I hope?"

"I hope I am."

"You must go. You'll adore it, I promise."

Her mother interjected. "I'm against it, Robin. I hear they're stoning the English in Peru."

"Oh, they're not stoning the English, Ma! That's rubbish."

Robin rocked back in his chair, looking surprised and most amused. "It's not as bad as that, is it?" he said, with a short reassuring laugh. "Is that what Hunt says? It certainly hasn't been my experience. Lima is a magnificent city. Of course, there's appalling poverty in Latin America, and I expect you're right that there will be trouble soon but they still need us."

"Well, I sense he's ready to come back and I'd feel much happier with him here." Eleanor's mother couldn't be doing with abroad. "He sounds very homesick all of a sudden in his letters. I think he'd like to come home and start a business in Liverpool."

"Would he? Here?"

Eleanor's father nodded. "Dicey, Liverpool, now."

Robin turned to Eleanor again. "Hunt lives in a marvellous place, all glass, with a breathtaking view of the city. You'd have a fantastic holiday. His parties are legendary." His eyes were wistful at the memory. "Everybody in Lima longs for an invitation."

"Right," she said, "I'm going then. Oh, Ma, I've got to go!"

"If you'd like an escort for the journey, I'm always ready to oblige!" He turned to her mother with another of his divinely reassuring smiles. "Would that seem safe enough? I go to Peru fairly regularly on business for my father."

A few days later, Eleanor received a little book from him full of pictures of Lima.

"Men like Robin Stewart White don't grow on trees," her mother said.

After that he was invited to her coming out dance. To her surprise he came. He didn't dance much. He stood on the sidelines, among two or three stiff, silent wallflowers, looking amiable and older and above it all. The dinner jacket seemed to emphasise his startlingly white hair. Robin Stewart White was the object of several secret prayers and longing glances from the ballroom floor. Automatically, Eleanor picked him first in a snowball because that was her duty as a hostess. But she wasn't thinking about him. She was trying not to cry because the band had just refused to play in the dark so they'd ruined her dance. A couple of cheek to cheek tunes with the lights out were as vital a part of the programme at all the dances as the charleston. She'd wanted hers to be the most sensational band ever. Instead, her dance was going to be the disaster of the year.

She couldn't hear what he was saying. She was only aware of a horrible whining violin rising and falling for a slow waltz and the massed ranks of formal, forlorn figures, waiting to join in the catastrophically leaden dancing.

She couldn't look at Robin because she felt such a fool.

He bent at the knees, forcing her to meet his eyes. "You look like a tulip," he said cheerily above the music, then he twirled her round and round so the golds and yellows of her dress swirled into one glorious sunset of colour.

"I didn't mean to look like one," she answered ungraciously, nearly dying because he felt sorry for her. "These blasted idiots can't play in the dark, I'm afraid."

His head jerked back as if, she thought, he reeled from her forwardness. "I'm relieved," he said quickly, twirling her again, "otherwise you might be invalided out. I don't think I could dance in the dark. Doesn't everybody bump into each other?"

She tried to think of some more things to say to him but couldn't think of anything elevated enough so they danced in silence.

He said, "You're not your uncle's niece, are you?" and the music stopped.

He paused with his polite smile, peered briefly into her soul, which he'd found wanting, then he made straight for Wheezy, her school friend from Evesham, as all the men had been doing all evening. Looking more blonde and original than ever, Wheezy Palmer had wound a hand-painted shawl around her slender body and painted her nails black. The result was a masterpiece of chic.

Seeing Robin Stewart White fall for it too was only the last straw. He didn't come back. Eleanor gave no further thought to him after the dance so she was surprised when he telephoned one day and invited her to go to a point-to-point near Tarporley. She was excited but the excitement was for the wrong reasons.

She was flattered because he was much older. She quite enjoyed her talks with Robin. More than that, she enjoyed being seen having conversations with him, and he flew his own aeroplane. The truth was, this dazzling figure belonged in another league. Only gradually, as a pattern for their meetings slowly began to emerge, did she realise how much she genuinely looked forward to seeing him. Whenever he came to the Liverpool office, they did something together. He took her racing at Chester or Haydock or they went to the theatre. New plays streamed into the Royal Court, in those days, on their way to London. Sometimes some of Robin's friends made up a party to have dinner and dance.

"I'm being accused of cradle snatching," he said after one of those dancing evenings at the Grosvenor in Chester.

It didn't seem to bother him although it bothered her. She brooded on these remarks. He'd showed them a photograph of himself, on a business trip, drinking champagne with Miss Canada. Somebody exclaimed in a teasing voice, 'Bit of a comedown after Miss Canada, isn't it, when you've got to start scratching about round here for a girlfriend!'

It was a joke but she pondered on it. She probably was a comedown from the people he met in London and other places. The trouble was she didn't feel nearly sure enough she was his girlfriend. He gave her flowers, he bought her chocolates and he'd sent her a jokey little valentine card but they were not making progress. Their meetings were romantic but without intimacy. They hovered on the brink of something deeper. But nothing happened.

So she waited, growing intense about everything, and less and less able to behave naturally because being herself wasn't enough. Each outing he organised was still smoothly perfect but months later they remained in first gear and she didn't seem able to find the right button. He was out of reach.

In between times, when he was away, she mused on their closest moments, considering them from every angle and analysing all the silences and penetrating looks. The moment she treasured most was from an evening when they were walking on the cliffs. The tide was disappearing, leaving all the little boats dotted against a red, darkening sky. She'd come flying out to meet him in a sagging old golf sweater of her father's and for once she hadn't spent hours at the mirror tinkering with her hair. The air was sharp, scented with seaweed and dewy grass from the links. A hundred times since in her thoughts she'd recreated that magical atmosphere. There was the lone, loud squawk of an occasional bird and the faintest rush of the receding water, as she listened tensely to her own voice, then his, cutting across the night silence.

He'd stopped, and laid his hands against the sides of her face. "I think you're the most beautiful girl I've ever seen," he said and kissed her. She didn't see him again for weeks.

Women always want more, men say. Women want more only because men don't give enough.

Eleanor tried out a well-rehearsed and probing little speech next time they were driving along in the car.

"Of course," she remarked musingly, as if an interesting

thought had suddenly occurred to her, "I've always thought it was important not to do anything until I absolutely felt something and was properly committed to someone. Have you made love to anyone, ever?" She paused for a second. "I suppose you have?"

There was a small surprised silence. She thought his admission came reluctantly. "I have, yes."

"Oh . . . yes, have you."

She looked out of the car window, wondering how she could find out who it was without actually asking for her name and address. Who could it be who was so loose? Had she got a bad name?

"Well, I . . . um . . . did you . . ." She cleared her throat and stopped.

What if Robin was still doing it with this loose one?

What if he loved her because she cared nothing for getting a bad name?

She turned anxiously, her mouth open to speak and her mind whirling. He only had the trace of a smile. "If you ever feel like making love," he said, in a smoothly fatherly tone, "let me know. I'm available any time you like."

They both laughed and she felt happier. She was touched he was being so respectful towards her. But that mood did not last long. What if he wanted her to make the decision for them so he was freed from all responsibility for feeling anything?

In her gloomiest moods, she went over all the gaffes she'd made which might have been detrimental to the closeness of their relationship, considering his age and old Etonian social standing. The worst was right at the beginning when a waiter asked her how she would like her steak done and she'd thought frantically about methods of cooking and eventually said 'Grilled'. The waiter nodded.

Good God. It made her go hot to think about it. *That waiter nodded and made a note.* Neither he nor Robin gave so much as a flicker of amusement. Hugo would have gone on guffawing all the way home.

She'd met Hugo by then. He lived nearby. He was a callow youth, not long home from school in Switzerland where he'd been sent because of his asthma. He wore a trilby on the back of his head and loped about under the name of Lucky Morrow because he intended to be a conjuror. All the time he was talking, he had a pack of cards fanning like a ribbon up and down his arm. Eleanor found his manner strangely insolent and continental.

He often invited her to his house for tea. They had Fullers walnut cake and ate the lot. No displays of dainty feminine restraint were necessary for him.

What particularly annoyed her was his attitude to Robin Stewart White, whom he'd only met in passing anyway, when she introduced them. He missed no opportunity to be rude about him.

She dropped Eton into the conversation as often as she could to crush him into a respectful state.

"The English public school system is dedicated to mediocrity, dullness and homosexuality," he responded contemptuously. "If they saw a spark of imaginative ability, they'd crush it. Boys are being cloned into rip-off lawyers and accountants, that's all."

"Robin works for his father. They've got offices everywhere," she explained crossly. "The whole point of Eton is that it encourages individuals. Actually, that place produces the leaders of tomorrow," she added, using a phrase she'd just seen in the *News Chronicle*.

Hugo manipulated the ace of hearts along the backs of his long fingers. "Those old boy businessmen. They've been going out and diddling the foreigners for years. How d'you think people got those huge houses? The English middle class is as offensive a breed as anything on the face of this earth."

Mothers, Eleanor's among them, saw Hugo Hobbs as a bad influence and put it down to the lack of a father. His father had died suddenly while he was at prep school.

"They say they're going to make it up to you," he said, "but they never do. They just forget about you." Mrs Hobbs hadn't made it up to him. She was always away at dog shows winning prizes with her reeking Bedlingtons.

Eleanor could tell that raw little boy was still in there minding the let-down. He didn't shine at school as his elder brother Edward and his sister Marian had. He was a loner. He ran away. He relived it all for Eleanor because his descriptions made her laugh but she could picture the upset of it at the time. She could imagine the small taciturn figure putting on his school cap and setting out to walk all the miles home.

After his father died, Hugo told her, his mother developed a mouth mannerism. Whenever she'd finished saying something, her lower jaw jutted out in a tortured biting movement.

Her little boy copied her. Oblivious in their sorrow, the distressed pair were doing it together. When Hugo went back to school, the music mistress, Miss Penkett-Moore, pounced at once on the new habit. "My goodness me, Hobbs, we'll soon get you out of that," she promised, throwing her head back and squaring her shoulders.

He took her down with him. Weeks later, towards the end of term, Miss Penkett-Moore was on duty in the dining room. She waited until the assembled boys were standing silently behind their chairs then she closed her eyes for Grace. "For what we are about to receive, may the Lord make us truly thankful," she said. Her jaw jutted in a terrible biting movement and the whole school did it after her.

What was happening of course was that Eleanor could not help using Hugo. He was the stuff of everyday life. She was spending time with him while she waited for Robin Stewart White, who was the stuff of dreams. "My uncle's business friend," she called him, implying that she had some role to play in that respect and hoping that Hugo would not be hurt.

It was a relief that Uncle Hunt was coming home soon on three months' leave. Whenever she saw Robin, it would seem as if there was some excuse for it.

As it turned out, she saw less of him while Hunt was staying. Robin flew him from London in his plane and he arrived in the usual flurry of presents and excitement.

Eleanor sniffed that familiar bedroom smell again with pleasure, marvelling at the neat array of silver and pigskin on the dressing table, unlike her father who had clumps of crumpled clothes scattered about his dressing room and a chest of drawers awash with pools coupons, betting notes on old envelopes and screwed-up cigarette packets.

Uncle Hunt wasn't around a lot of the time because he kept speeding away to spend a few days in London. When he was at home he had a cup of coffee at eleven o'clock then he set off, stoutly spruce in his bow tie, to lunch in Liverpool with his cronies. He always arrived back a bit late for supper, shouting "What ho, Norming!" as he came up the drive.

"He's picklecake," Norman Mackie observed mildly, each time, opening the window a fraction to greet him. "Hallo, Hunt."

But he took to sidling stealthily to his wife's side for *sotto voce* grumbling. "I'm getting awfully sick of it. Why does he call me Norming? It's so silly. Oh *hell*, he hasn't had the water heater on again, has he?" He'd groan and jab his finger towards the ceiling as sounds of running water were heard from upstairs. "He's still tight after we've had our meal, that's what's infuriating. He talks back to the television, grunting 'Rubbish. Drop dead!' and that sort of thing, then he passes out and snores like a grampus. You'll have to tell him we don't want him snoring while we're watching television."

"The drinking's worse than ever this time," Eleanor's mother agreed. "I've warned him but I think we'll have to hold our peace so as not to spoil his last few days. There's only the theatre trip to *Salad Days* and then he goes back to South America for three years."

Eleanor was setting a lot of store on this *Salad Days* evening in which Robin Stewart White was to be included. At least Uncle Hunt was never intimidated by the rich or anybody else. He'd be his usual rollicking self which would give her more confidence and that should be the key to making some headway in her relationship with Robin.

Unfortunately, Hunt was not his usual self. He was a bit drunk and in rather a disagreeable mood. It put a damper on the outing from the start. Eleanor's father stayed behind because he only stirred himself for visits from the D'Oyly Carte or holiday treats to the Edinburgh Tattoo. Robin insisted on taking them all to dinner beforehand and it was the beginning of those strange nightmares connected with him.

Uncle Hunt did not eat much. He took a few mouthfuls in a half-hearted manner then he pushed his plate away. He said very little during the meal until Eleanor's mother glanced at the menu and remarked, "Oh, look, Nella, here's our favourite . . . apple pie!" After that he kept on saying "Applee pee!", butting his head and making aggressive little gruff mooing noises with his mouth closed. Eleanor didn't know whether it was better to look at him or look away. He was staring round with his eyes wide and his mouth squashed out as if he'd been hit on the head with a sledge hammer. It made a most awkward atmosphere. She couldn't tell what Robin was thinking but her mother was looking strained and darting dagger glances.

Hunt didn't care for the wildly successful *Salad Days*. It may have been too delicate for his taste or, more likely, he resented sitting through it without a drink. When the interval came, he said, "Ooh, what a stinker!" and he was on his way to the bar before the others had even stood up. He was waiting with their drinks when they joined him.

There was such a crush, and so much enthusiastic chat about the performance, that Eleanor was hardly aware of her uncle. She heard her mother issuing one of her grim warnings to him, "It always gets back!" and as the bell went, Robin said, "For God's sake, Hunt!" his mouth twitching with exasperation. It wasn't until they were back in their seats and the orchestra had already struck up for the second half, that she realised he hadn't come with them. He'd stayed in the bar.

Eleanor adored *Salad Days*. She'd known all the tunes for ages and she was waiting for each one. The whole audience was enraptured. Suddenly, something made her turn her head and her heart sank. Uncle Hunt was standing over by one of the side exits, glowering round the auditorium.

"Lee dee dee . . . lee dee dee . . ." piped the youthful voices on the stage, singing to the tinkling music, about looking for a piano.

His head on one side, Huntly Quinton plucked up the corners of his jacket as if about to curtsey. He pointed his toe.

Moving on tiptoe, he did a little dancing run down the right-hand aisle and along in front of the seats in the front row. He paused in front of the orchestra pit to conduct, with a raised forefinger. He looked, from behind, like Mr Toad.

"Get off!" he said malevolently to the people on the stage.

Eleanor could hardly believe it was happening. The actors carried on, and the audience went on watching them. Robin's hand was across his forehead, shielding his face. "How could he do this to us?" her mother murmured.

"You!" Quinton bellowed, pointing over the heads of the orchestra. "You're awful. I want you off." He made a sweeping dismissive movement with his arm towards the wings. "Get out of it! And don't call us!"

Eleanor couldn't move. It was like a bad dream. Her arm wouldn't move and her mouth was stuck. Out of the corner of her eye, she saw an attendant coming. Her mother zoomed down the aisle and beat him to it.

"Get back to your seat," she hissed furiously, tweaking at her brother's arm. "Sit down at once."

"I'm sorry, Sir," the attendant said, "I shall have to ask you to leave if you cause a disturbance during the performance."

"Quite right," Huntly Quinton replied, in a reasonable voice. "It won't happen again." He sat down and stared ahead with a composed expression of pleasant anticipation.

The temptation was too much. It happened almost immediately. "You . . ." he said to someone on the stage, "Yes, *you*! You're a bloody broken-down cow. That's what you are. I don't like you one little bit!" He stood up as the attendant bore down again. "All right!" he called, "I'm coming quietly."

Eleanor wasn't surprised that that episode temporarily put paid to Robin's visits. She felt wounded when there was no explanation for his silence but she could imagine how appalled he was. He was so controlled himself. Hunt's display would be incomprehensible to him.

"I don't blame Robin," her mother said. "We were absolutely disgraced that evening. People get sick to death of drinkers. They spoil everything."

"Going out with Robin is wrecked now."

"He will get in touch again, I'm sure of that, but he's a dark horse. You don't really know him, do you?"

Eleanor wasn't admitting that. She pined inwardly. She remembered herself hanging round the kitchen door while her mother stirred pans and basted the meat in the oven. She droned round and round the subject of Robin White until they were both exhausted by the sound of his name.

That was her first experience of Hunt's drinking doing damage. Of course it wasn't the last.

Now, she thought, in middle age, she'd know how to deal with a dark horse. But who could be bothered with one?

If she was going to meet Robin when she went to the hospital each day, how could she fail to get to know him? They'd be stuck there together thinking of gossip to cheer up Hunt. They'd mull his situation over when they were alone and then, inevitably, they'd mull their own. How ironical. She was to get what she'd wanted. Years too late.

But of course it was nonsense, she reminded herself, as she stopped the car on a grass verge, to put on more lipstick and make her skin gleam with youthful moisture.

Robin wouldn't be anywhere near the hospital. He never had been. It was Uncle Hunt's fantasy. He wanted to make amends.

He was sitting smoking with Evelyn and Ada when she arrived that afternoon. "What ho, sweet!" he said, reaching out thin arms to embrace her, "I am glad to see you. You have to be tough as a goat and slippery as a snake to survive in this place."

She laughed. "How are you feeling today?"

"I'm all right, thank you, Nella. I've got one or two problems to deal with, you know. You've just missed Robin White. He sent his love to you."

Chapter 4

Liverpool, Eleanor already knew, had become a ghost town. Nearly all the big shops, like the Bon Marché, where her mother asked for bust bodices and nigger-brown twin sets (on appro), were gone. The city part, down by the water, had an empty deserted air. There weren't many cars on the streets and all the signs she remembered of middle class life must have vanished as long ago as Fullers and the North John Street Kardomah, which used to be one of her lunchtime haunts. In her grandfathers' time, Liverpool bustled like London. Now, it looked bashed and bereft, like the morning after the night before. That same wayward spirit of its people, which must have worked for good when there were resources like shipping and cotton to make it prosperous, had brought about its destruction when these were gone. Nobody would dream of taking a business to Liverpool now. It had destroyed itself.

And yet her friends, some of them, lived on in their big houses and their lives continued the same as ever. They went on organising Conservative lunches, raising money for charity and playing golf four afternoons a week. Having a career might not have got to them but they'd got to grips with the Welfare State. A word like dole had slipped into their vocabularies as naturally as breathing.

She had rung one or two people, the ones she'd kept in touch with all along, and, of course, Hugo's sister, Marian, who'd married into an old Liverpool printing family at twenty-one and stayed put to become Ladies Captain at the golf club. She didn't see anybody else. She drove about almost in a dream, staring up at houses where she'd been to dance or to play tennis. She was pretending the same families were still in there and that she could resume life where she'd left off, riding on the shore and playing ping-pong with her father and Uncle Victor on Sunday nights. Some of the houses no longer existed. Her father's old home had been knocked down and flats built instead. Others remained for sale month after month because there was nobody coming into the area to buy them.

It was the same place and yet it wasn't the same at all. She wanted to belong, but the waters had closed over her head, and she no longer did. If she waited . . . waited for what? For Uncle Hunt? For her mother to come back? For Robin?

"How are you getting on?" Hugo asked, when he rang after coming back from France.

"Okay. I can't get the nurses to say much about Hunt's state. I suppose they have to speak with optimism. Sometimes he talks sense and other times he's right off his rocker. All I can say is if it ever happens to me, I'm taking morphine and dying of gangrene. Did you get on well?"

"Not really," he replied in a weary disgruntled voice, meant to underline his lone state, "I feel I'm fighting off the Indians here. I've got arrows coming from all sides, what with this house and all our bills and Hunt's leg. I find the antique world so depressing. You can get a deal out of a man who's made money himself but the man who inherits is as tight as shit. He behaves as if it's an affront to the face of God if anybody else makes tuppence out of him. I've been waiting on tenterhooks on at least three pieces."

"Something always happens."

"Yes, but how soon? When I was in Kensington High Street this morning, I opened one of those 'Come in Boat 9' letters in yobbo-speak from the Bank Manager. My neck locked. I had double vision. I thought I was going to be knocked down."

Eleanor put her hand across her mouth so she didn't laugh immoderately. Hugo heard the strangled sound and laughed too.

"People don't want antiques, that's what you've got to remember. The person buying these days has capped teeth and leisure clothes and what they want is something they can refer to as an Elizabethan coffer when it's actually a spanking new chest. Medieval furniture has to do with religion, which they don't like, and it wobbles. There's only one sort of bourgeois kit they all go for. That's made up of a dresser, a refectory table and a set of ghastly chairs, with what they call carvers, so that Mr and Mrs Yuppie can sit at each end of their fake table in their ill-begotten house."

"Mmm . . ." She was thinking about them and their category.

"You can imagine the greedy gabbling of the dealer, can't you, when I come to sell your mother's wine cooler? '*Yis!*' He switched to a whining and offended tone. 'Who wants the old-fashioned wine coolers?' he'll be saying, 'They've all got fridges now.'"

She drew a sunflower on her mother's new telephone book, "What I wanted to sa . . ."

"If you arrived with the *Mona Lisa*," Hugo continued, brightening up at the thought of it, "the dealer would take one look and throw his arms out. 'Nice,' he'd say, 'Very nice but *smiling*. Women, yes, but where's the market for smiling?' He'd shrug. 'There is a market, I suppose? I don't know the people. I'd have to try and find them.' He'd step back then, and shake his head with a derogatory laugh. 'Smiling women . . . no. I'm very sorry. I don't see it. It could sit here for five years. If you'd come ten years ago, who can say? But *now*. Who wants the smiles?'"

She needn't have worried. He wasn't giving a thought to their marital situation. Hugo amused her when she was two hundred miles away. It was when she was with him she couldn't stop being angry. Their existence was already fading into a haze of huge, late meals, drowned by Jelly Roll Morton, Hugo's soliloquies concerning builders, antique dealers and leathery women, and the sound of more slates crashing off the roof.

That house was the root of their troubles. It was too big, cost too little and they'd been spending a fortune on it ever since. Hugo insisted on brass taps, marble basins and stolen fireplaces so they sat hunched in a huge dusty, empty shell surrounded by some pieces of spectacularly rare furniture, two thousand jazz records, and an attic full of escape cabinets and magic tricks, while builders banged on, piercing water pipes, stepping through ceilings, demanding more and more money and bailiffs hammered at the door. She was sick of chaos, that was all. Bed and Breakfast. What a joke. She wanted to lie down for a hundred years at the thought of it.

Respectability was what she'd been expecting. Hugo didn't know the meaning of the word whereas her childhood had been overflowing with it. She'd thought Liverpool was heaven then. Better than anywhere. Kinder, livelier. Now it was worse. More drug-ridden, more deserted. Old landmarks remained, but sitting isolated, dotted round the huge hole where the heart had been. Even theatres were closed because late night trains were too frightening. Respectable was a redundant word when society's respected were those who got away with it. Something happened to her in a shop which mirrored the hollow, hopeless atmosphere.

Some mornings Eleanor walked to a small, ill-stocked corner shop which was showing all the signs of imminent collapse. Prices were staggeringly high and the organic vegetables displayed neither abundant nor particularly fresh.

This time she was alone for a moment in the shop because the woman had disappeared into her back room to get some change. The door opened and two big, well-built young men swaggered in, obtrusively filling the remaining space. Eleanor had time for faint surprise. The shop sold no cigarettes on principle. They were not the usual retired customers.

"Excuse me, madam."

She turned round.

"We're police officers, madam. We'd like a word with you."

"Yes?" she answered. She was aware of the door opening again to admit a third man.

"We have reason to believe you have been working while drawing unemployment benefit."

"What?"

"We have reason to believe you have been working whilst obtaining fraudulent Social Security payments and we would like you to accompany us to the station to answer a few questions."

"*What!*" her mind was reeling with shock. She was so

used to trouble. Was it the Council writ? The rates? Was it mistaken identity?

"We understand you have a job, madam? Our information is you've been receiving Social Security payments whilst working as well."

It was like a nightmare. She felt guilty. She was aghast. She looked from the two men to the third. A hundred years seemed to pass. All were silently watching her.

"D'you have a job, madam?"

"I have a job," she replied aggressively, terrified of enmeshing herself in this incomprehensible web, "but I don't live here." Had they followed her from London? "What are you talking about?"

"Lost your bottle, didn't you?"

"What . . .?" she said, leaning forward incredulously, "What?"

The men were triumphant. "You lost your bottle there. We had you for a moment! Fell for that one, didn't you, love?"

The third man spoke up. "Impersonating police officers is a criminal offence." He held the door open for Eleanor. "You'd better watch yourselves. Next time you could be in real trouble."

Outside, he walked some yards along the pavement with her until they were out of sight and earshot.

"I'm very grateful," she said. "What an awful joke."

"I guessed they were up to some trick like that. I saw them stopping people down by the supermarket."

"But are you a policeman?"

His whole body swayed with amusement. "Have a heart! I'm nothing to do with it. I was passing, that's all. This place is so run down, it's their idea of a huge joke to give people a heart attack about the DHSS. A lot of

72

Merseysiders wouldn't survive at all without drawing the dole and working as well."

"I'm not on the dole." She felt a need to explain, still embarrassed. "I don't even live here now but I felt rattled. I imagined some fearful long-drawn-out case of mistaken identity and how I'd never get out of it."

"It's a pity you didn't insist on going to the police station. That's what they need. Come over the road and have a drink," he suggested, gesturing towards the Red Lion. "Forget it."

"No, no . . . really," she replied hastily, stepping back. "I don't want to be a nuisance. You were in the middle of shopping."

"Come on. I'm going to have one."

She hesitated. He was a youngish man with attractive thyroidal eyes. There wouldn't be anything to talk about. She would look ridiculous if any more was made of this incident.

"No. I won't, thanks. I've got a hospital visit to make and I'd better go and get on with it. Thank you very much. I expect we'll meet again . . . round about." She laughed to bestow a casual warmth on that prospect and walked off.

It was rather extraordinary. After that, she did see him. Not once but practically every day. Even if they didn't actually meet, he seemed to appear wherever she went.

She saw him behind her in a queue of cars waiting at lights on the Chester Road. She turned round and bumped into him in the fish shop and when she came out of Hugo's sister, Marian's, house one afternoon later in that week, he was sitting in his car reading a newspaper.

Much amused, she tapped on the window as she walked past. "Who's doing the following? You or me?"

"What about our drink?" he said pleasantly.

She unlocked the door and climbed into her car, then she drove slowly past his car and lowered the window. "You be careful or I might take you up on it," she said, laughing, and drove off.

'An agreeable little man for someone to talk to,' she was thinking as she accelerated away, 'but it won't be me.'

When she sighted him in the hospital car park the following day, she was too dumbfounded to say a word. She pretended not to see him.

"I've almost begun to believe I've got somebody following me," she said to Marian, when they were chatting on the telephone.

"Who?"

"Well, I don't know who. He's just ordinary, athletic-looking . . . quite handsome in a way with a lot of thick dark hair." She told her what had happened in the shop. "Oh, and fairly young. About thirty-five or eight or so."

"My dear, how bloody flattering. Lucky you!"

"Are you interested in the young? I'm not."

"All passion spent in my case, I fear," Marian admitted in her rather languid voice, "I don't suppose I'd recognise a cock if I saw one. I only think about death these days. Can Hugo still get it up?"

"Actually he doesn't attempt to which doesn't worry me. I believe it's a myth that people go on being interested in sexual intercourse. Menopausal pamphlets are published with bright-eyed women promising it gets better than ever. But how can it? I mean apart from boredom, we all get dropped wombs and ballooning of the abdomen and dry up like prunes, drenched in sweat. Now we know why people start saying 'Disgusting!' about sexual matters. I suppose all one can hope to hold onto in old age is dignity."

With hearty laughter, the two women mused on the appalling fate in store.

"The ghastliness of the menopause," Marian explained, "is that nobody tells you what to expect. When I asked Mummy about it, she told me she couldn't remember what it was like except her face got bigger. She said women either went through it without noticing or they went crackers and there could be incontinence."

"Oh my God." Eleanor could imagine her saying it. Hermione Hobbs had been an angular woman, with a voice like a corncrake, who smoked a pipe and did an impressive charleston into her seventies.

"She called it The Change," Marian went on, "and she started to make bracing references to it at every opportunity, warning me that anybody who used hormone replacement therapy ended up looking like Bugs Bunny.

"I had one perfectly frightful shopping expedition with her. I was flaked out on a chair, with my head spinning, while Mummy tried on one thing after another and changed her mind about everything. She suddenly pointed at me, drawing me to the assistant's attention. 'My daughter's gone giddy in The Change!' I wanted to go through the floor."

Marian and Eleanor had always laughed together. Sometimes they didn't speak for months at a stretch but there was always some family event to swing them back in touch. They'd pick up where they left off except that Marian had invariably moved on to captain the golf club ladies or attend a Buckingham Palace garden party or hold a respectfully attended exhibition of her pressed flower pictures in their domed glass frames.

"My dear, I don't know what you're going to do about this follower. He sounds most alarming to me. Oughtn't you to tell the police? Of course, if he were a rapist, he'd hardly go to so much trouble, would he, when he could just leap out on you from behind a tree?"

"I'm going to tell him to push off," Eleanor said.

It wasn't long before she had the opportunity. Next time she went to the hospital, he drove into the park as she was getting out of her car. Her chest bumped with shock. 'Right!' she thought.

"Look." She didn't bother with preliminaries as she approached his car window. "My name is Hobbs. I don't know your name. I don't know who you are but I am beginning to wonder why everywhere I go, I find you there as well?"

He gave her a buoyant smile. "It's about time you called me Eric."

"If that's what everybody else calls you . . . well, no . . ." She swivelled on her feet, seeking appropriate words. "Actually I don't think . . . what I mean to say is I don't really expect to be calling you anything, because nobody can stand being followed about like this."

"Haven't I as much right to be in the hospital car park as you have?"

"May I ask who you're visiting?"

"No business of yours, is it, if I choose to visit Mr Quinton?"

She gasped with irritation, turned away and went stalking down the path towards the geriatric wards. How did he know Hunt's name? Of course, he probably knew all kinds of things about her by now. He could be watching the house. What on earth was he playing at?

When her telephone rang at ten o'clock that evening, she knew who it was going to be. She felt relieved there were no pips.

"Hello, Hobbs," he said.

"We've said all we've got to say." Despite her fierce voice, she shivered.

"No we haven't. I want to talk to you properly. Can I come round?"

"I should have to call the police."

"I can bring the police with me."

"This doesn't amuse me, you know. I will tell the police about you. I'm sorry to do it because I was extremely grateful to you for standing up for me in that shop. But I do not want to find you everywhere I go."

"Well come and have a drink with me then."

She hesitated. A quick drink might be the best solution if that was going to be the end of it.

"All right," she suggested with an ill grace, "I could meet you down the road at the Red Lion."

They made an arrangement for six o'clock the following day. "See you soon then, Hobbs," he said.

'What a damn bore,' she thought, putting the telephone down. 'I don't even see the people I know. Now I'm wasting my time with somebody I'm not remotely interested in who could easily turn out to be a well-known nutter.'

She skulked resentfully along the road to the pub the next evening, hoping not to meet anybody she knew. When she went up to the bar to get a drink, she found he was there already.

"Hallo, Hobbs, what do you drink?"

"Whisky with ice, please."

He paid for their drinks and led the way to a mercifully secluded corner by the window. He was a bit too glossily dressed in the mode of the moment in what Hugo contemptuously called leisure clothes, although the touching thing about him was the mixture of swagger and gaucherie. She sat down, trying to bring an agreeable expression on to her face.

She lifted her glass, without smiling. "With thanks for your help."

"Cheers." He drank gingerly because of the froth on his pint of beer.

She waited.

"How's your uncle?"

She resisted the temptation of expressing surprise that he didn't already know. She described Hunt's condition and how she'd come back from London to look after him.

"How long are you going to stay here?"

"As long as it takes," she said, being deliberately vague, "I don't know when my mother will be back."

Their meeting was more successful than she'd anticipated. He was in Liverpool collecting statistics for a research survey. The conversation wasn't laborious. He made no attempt to explain himself although he asked her a great many questions. In fact, he appeared so straightforward and genuinely interested, she found it embarrassing to ask why he'd been following her.

"I like you."

"Surely you could go about things in a more normal manner?"

"You wouldn't have taken any notice."

"No."

"You're married, I see, Hobbs?"

"Yes."

"What's gone wrong?"

"Nothing."

"Nothing?" His eyes narrowed in an irritatingly exaggerated way, "What are you doing here then?"

"Doing my duty."

"I've booked a table for us to eat in Liverpool."

"You must be *joking*! Oh, I don't want to go lumping through the tunnel to Liverpool."

"Come on, Hobbs, you're not doing anything else. It's a smashing place. I like talking to you. Please come."

The place wasn't smashing. It was a down-at-heel club in a poky smoky room with a tiny bar at one end and one or two desultory drinkers clustered round it, saying 'What's your poison?' to each other. They went next door to eat and sat side by side in semi-darkness on a sunken moquette-covered bench.

It was an amazing evening. She went on being annoyed with him for assuming she would go out and annoyed with herself for going. But he didn't look or act like a madman. He hung upon her words, obviously fascinated. She hoped she wasn't moon-faced, beside this younger man, like Hugo's mother after the menopause. There was a feeling of imminent incontinence which she attributed to stress.

"Tell me what your husband's like?"

"Hugo," she considered, "is quite often away these days although he's actually rather home-minded. Well, he's difficult. On the surface he is anyway but he's got worthwhile depths. What I mean is, he might work himself into a fury about, say, something remote like . . . um, cleansing the Church of England of rotten bishops. That's one of his favourites. He never goes to church of course except to look at the furniture or the carving.

"Hugo would laugh to himself at the thought of tucking up somebody rich with a frightful fake, but he's the one, you know, who'll race a stray animal to the vet, wait about all day and pay a fortune for it. He's all mouth but

79

he does have something most special in the ... er ...
knickers, as they say," she concluded, laughing.

"What's he doing when he's away?"

"God knows. Arranging his antique deals ... seeing
magic acts. He goes off and looks at things. I've known
him take off for Persia in the past just to look at a medieval
mosque. His languages are good because he went to school
in Switzerland. The trouble is we're not rich. I think he
lives in a sort of dream. He lives in the manner that his
family was accustomed to and we can't afford."

"D'you go with him?"

"He never asks me. I used to mind. But we've got a dog
and I've got a job. He'll drop everything, if you can believe
it, to see an act he admires performing somewhere. He
went to Las Vegas last year to see Siegfried and Roy. Hugo
invites magicians to stay when they're in London and they
spend hours closetted in the attic showing each other
tricks. He used to perform himself, you see. His first wife,
Barbara, was a dancer from Morecambe so she was his
assistant."

"Barbara came on in shimmering bikinis, did she?" His
eyes moved over her figure as if ruling out that possibility
in her case.

"Bowing and beaming while the most appalling rows
went on in the dressing room. Hugo's marvellous at
magic. A genius really but he gave it all up because he says
conjurors never top the bill and he got sick of working in
clubs. I felt he hated the audience. The people bored him."

Once she'd started talking about Hugo, she couldn't
stop. It didn't matter. Her marriage in its current state had
all but had it anyway and airing it helped her to detach.
"Hugo and I are beyond speech, that's our trouble. We've
become good friends." She was enjoying Eric's rapt atten-

tion. She'd forgotten what being taken out was like. She hadn't gone out and been chatted up for years.

His long looks and loud applauding laughs were most exhilarating but by the end of the evening she only felt venerated. And old. He had a youthful zest which wearied her. Anyway, she wasn't looking for an affair and, if she had been, he wasn't suitable. She found him eminently resistible. He was quite ordinary.

"Do you and Hugo give each other freedom within your marriage?"

"Freedom to commit adultery? Good Lord, no."

"You never have?"

"Never."

"I've warned the people I'm staying with I won't be home tonight."

"They're in for a happy surprise then, aren't they."

For a minute it seemed as if he'd lost heart at last. There was a long silence. She was at a loss as to how to fill it.

Under the table, to her horror, something pressed against her thigh.

"I can be quite witty, you know, Hobbs."

"I'm sure you can." Poor little soul. What *was* he doing? She glanced down. *Good God!* He'd got it out. "And is this a small example of your wit?" she said. It was huge.

With a dawning dread she knew she was not going to see the last of him when the evening ended. She stated firmly that her circumstances were too complicated and that her husband would not understand. Also, since she was nearly ten years older, she felt old enough to be his mother, a feeling she did not relish. She might have saved her breath.

He rang her the next day. Every time he rang she put the telephone down. Instantly, he dialled again. "You don't understand," she told him crisply. "Women outgrow men.

At my age, they've had enough of them. I'm not interested in the man-woman situation."

"Come off it. Everybody is."

"You don't imagine I read books about that sort of thing, do you? I don't want to read about humdrum greedy deadbeats having so-called glamorous adventures and jerking off. My own search is for religious philosophies and something more satisfying."

"I can satisfy you, Hobbs. Just give me one night."

"Don't be ridiculous. Now listen to me, little fellow. I want you to grasp this. What women want from men may be children or houses or marital status or passion. They are not as romantic as men are. Young men are extremely idealistic and romantic. Women are not. They seem to choose the life they want with relentless practicality. It's only later, when men have made them very angry and disappointed, that they start searching for a meaning and spiritual fulfilment."

"You're wrong, Hobbs. I can't speak for the older woman of course but young girls are idealistic. They channel their idealism into their choice of mate. Children bring them spiritual fulfilment."

"Well, that's what you like to say. What I'm saying is that women blossom in middle age while many men . . . not you, I do hope," she said, smiling to herself, "turn into husks. On their deathbeds, men go back to babyhood. They look to the woman in their dotage as their mother, and that's how she dies, unsupported, alone and full of wisdom."

He gave one of his loud laughs.

"I've got to go."

"Kisses," said Eric Clover.

They were addictive, the conversations. She found

herself planning delicious shocks for when he rang (often a quote from Hugo's more outrageous ravings). She'd hear an astonished gasp at the other end and then listen to him rally gamely. As time went on she began to be disappointed when there was no call from him for her to torpedo.

She didn't mention anything to Hugo but Marian wanted to know what had happened to her mystery follower.

"We had a drink. I told him I was married. That's all."

"Did you find out why he was following you?"

"Marian, I know one can hardly presume at forty-four . . . how can I put this . . . that somebody has . . . er . . . caught a glimpse, as it were, and been . . . um . . . bewitched."

Her sister-in-law laughed. "My dear, just your sort of romantic . . ."

"Don't be silly. I probably imagined he was following when it was only a coincidence. There's no mystery. He's visiting the area for work and he's lonely. He rings me the whole time and I tell him to get lost. He's so bouncy and persistent, it makes me quite savage. I find it most therapeutic to be able to say anything that comes into my head. It doesn't matter, you know, how rude or outrageous it is. Nothing puts him off."

"Shall I meet him?"

"You could do but you wouldn't be interested. Oh, he's nothing, I'm afraid, my admirer, except, he's got marvellous dark thyroidal eyes and lustrous curly hair and a loud rollicking laugh. Instrusiveness is his strongest characteristic. Anyway, I don't let him come to the house. I'm not getting into that. Good Lord no."

"He's not a gigolo, is he?"

"Well thanks. If he is, he's come to the wrong person. He hasn't asked for money yet but maybe he's working up to it."

It was as if he'd overheard their conversation. The next day he was waiting, parked in the road outside the house, when she returned from the hospital. He had a plant for Uncle Hunt. Weakening, she asked him if he would like a drink.

She knew she was starting something which could become a habit, and did. It didn't matter though because when she'd had enough of him, she threw him out. She made no effort to entertain him. He lolled on the sofa, calling out to her, as she went about her business in the house.

He was making sexual suggestions as he watched her dusting. "When are you going to kiss me, Hobbs?"

She flicked the duster in his face then she moved along the windowsills picking up the vases and dusting underneath. "Never."

"Can't I kiss you?"

"Don't be silly and don't keep calling me Hobbs."

"But how am I to get on with you?"

"There's no need to get on with me."

"But I want to. I don't know how to get through to you."

Eleanor sat down on the edge of a chair. "To my amazement, you don't know what women are like, do you? If you ask a woman for permission to kiss her, all you're going to get is certain rejection."

She stared at him, thinking hard, as she tried to work out what she wanted to say. "Okay, you're attractive in a physical way. Right? You've got it all, *physically*. You're a sexual plum. What I mean is, if you behaved in certain mental ways, if say, I was involved with you . . . I would not be able to resist. I would fall into your power. No, no, you know that, of course, don't you? How embarrassing to be talking like this! These are games which no decent person would get up to. Are you laughing at me?"

He wasn't laughing. "Go on. Tell me."

"All right, I will. Remember, I'm only talking on the most shallow sexual level but women, I'm sorry to say it about my own sex, are lethal. Any idea that they respond to kindness is out. If the jugular is exposed, they go for it.

"They'll respond like anything once you've tipped them off balance and they're in your power. You've got to brainwash them. You've got to blow hot . . . show you need them, touch their hearts and then withdraw. Come back again, envelop with intensity while they're in a panic of longing, switch off and slide out of reach. It's torture, I suppose. Women won't admit it but that challenge is surefire. Remember, confidence is all in these games. Never lose the initiative and never admit it's a game. You are the iron man. Bluff to the last because women are killers. It's in their nature to manipulate till the man is under their heel then they step on him. D'you think you understand?"

"Let's try it."

She laughed. "Don't be silly. *We* won't try it. By Jove, no, not with our age gap. Do it on nubile women you meet."

"Sure," he said and she actually watched his face change and harden as if a mask had dropped over it.

She continued dusting, holding her stomach in and feeling matronly. "You're to stay as you are with me, please."

He came across. He put his hand under her chin and tilted her face up as iron men must have been doing to nubile girls through the ages and she felt thoroughly foolish. But her laughter faltered at the inhuman emptiness about his eyes.

Was it real? Was he acting? As he kissed her, she felt a delightful thrill of fright at the dangerous thing she had done.

"I don't want you to do it on me."

"It works better this way," he said.

After she'd slept with him, she found out he was a private eye. There were notes about her, addressed to Hugo, inside a book he was reading.

Eric Clover was staying at Uncle Hunt's digs. He hadn't told her that either.

Chapter 5

Huntly Quinton had ended up in digs when he lost all his money.

When he first came home from Peru to start an import/export business in Liverpool, he was loaded. He bought a desirable house and the new offices were sumptuous. There were super typewriters, super secretaries and stylish paintings on the walls. Some business too. Of course Uncle Hunt was already drinking and Liverpool already had the skids under it.

Cotton was finished and the docks were going the same way. Better tidal facilities lured ships into Southampton and cheaper labour in other countries put paid to local ship building.

There was constant trouble on the docks. The old firms, importing fruit and vegetables, had learned not to risk prolonged strikes while cargoes sat unloaded, going bad. They brought their goods into different ports and down to Livepool by road.

It could not be said that the dockers' container strikes alone ruined Hunt Quinton although they ruined others. For him, it was probably a combination of disasters coming all at once. A South American colleague swindled him out of a substantial amount of capital and he was either too worried or too tiddly to grasp what was going on.

Anyway, for a time he threw himself into Liverpool business life. He and Eleanor's father and Robin Stewart White joined up with a number of others to form an Investors' Club. Regular meetings to discuss strategy were held in an hotel room.

"He was picklecake," Norman Mackie observed to his family, more often than not, when he came home from one of the investors' meetings.

"The Chairman said, 'Mr Quinton, I believe export is your speciality? I wonder if you would care to say a few words to us about that.'

"He was beetle-browed and breathing down his nose as he does when he's watching television here," Eleanor's father reported. "Everybody waited, then he suddenly tossed the Investors' Club accounts up in the air so they scattered like confetti. He said, 'Never mind about export! Have you made any bloody money yet? That's what I want to know.'"

All the stages in her uncle's downfall were linked in Eleanor's memory to what was happening at the time in her relationship with Robin.

When Hunt was first back in England, she was still going to all her friends' dances. If she didn't sleep on till teatime the next day, she usually went riding, mooning along on Flora's fat black back, thinking about Robin White who was travelling round the world for his father. When she didn't hear from him, a suppurating red rash appeared on her neck. Her only decoration with her evening dress was the white bandage wound round and round to cover it up.

Uncle Hunt's business had collapsed and he had taken

over a sawdust pub in North Wales by the time she started her first job on the local paper.

She continued to go to dances but now they were held in town halls and municipal rooms and her mother stopped warning her never to let a man touch her bust. Eleanor had to produce the names of the organising committee and thirty dress descriptions to go into her glowing report.

Whether the bustling importance of the committee secretaries, the majestic dancing and the endless Babychams might have been too much for Stewart White was not put to the test. Hugo escorted her to most of these functions, and hung about while she did her job, hoping he might be called upon to supply an impromptu conjuring cabaret. He was already inventing his own tricks and writing articles for a magic magazine.

He did get a job eventually as a conjuror at a place in Liverpool. By day, it was the Bold Street Buffet for office workers' lunches and in the evening, with the help of some deep red drapes, it became the Changing Scene. The proprietor of the Changing Scene was a young cellist, fired from the Philharmonic, called Toby Broadbent. He hired Hugo Hobbs to go round all the diners' tables in a tail coat and entertain each one with an individual display of sleight of hand and jokes.

Eleanor waited until her parents had sat down for supper to break this splendid news. "Hugo's opening in intimate cabaret," he said. "He'd like us all to go and see him tomorrow night."

Her father's jaw dropped. "No, must we? What's it all going to come to in the end?" he added ungratefully. "That's what I wonder."

"He'll be a world famous conjuror, that's what, not like the boring people round here."

"Take your food to the mustard not the mustard to your food," her mother said.

"What if I want to know how much mustard I've got?"

"Don't you want to have any manners?"

"Where are manners going to get me? Hugo says they had manners in India while they were screwing everybody into the ground."

"Is he a socialist?" her father asked.

"Hugo has no manners," said Mrs Mackie. "If you raise your hat and open the door for people you never know where it will get you. Charm of manner can lead to anything."

"Look, I've told him you keep on saying that. He says it's horseshit. While he's standing there, raising his hat, bastards will be flocking past and slamming the door in his face."

Her mother shook her head, smiling faintly. "Poor Hugo. Anybody who says horseshit, of course, is damned for ever. Poor slouching boy, what a sight he is with that common hat on the back of his head. I only hope he won't be calling himself Lucky Morrow . . ." She let words fail her as she got up from the table.

Their evening at the Changing Scene was never to be forgotten.

When he didn't want to go anywhere, Eleanor noticed, her father could undermine and spread unease by his reluctant twitchy manner. He had a way of holding his head up and back, with the eyes rolling. It reminded her of the one time she'd seen him sitting on a bus, perched on the edge of the seat, like a cat on hot bricks.

They parked the car and walked down Bold Street. "Is it this dive?" he asked.

It was. There was a sandwich board outside announcing

90

an intimate cabaret with a big full-length picture of Lucky Morrow.

"*Poor thing,*" said Eleanor's mother.

Lucky was lunging forward to acknowledge what could only be tumultuous applause with a top hat in one outstretched hand and a spread of cards in the other. Eleanor's legs weakened momentarily at this exciting entry into the showbusiness world.

Inside the door of the Changing Scene, her father sniffed. "By jove, it's vinegar. What a stench!" he complained, fanning the air. "How disgusting. It's unpardonable, isn't it."

"Shhh . . ." said her mother, "Keep your voice down."

Bar two, all the tables were empty.

"Press night, I suppose," Mr Mackie observed, more benevolently. "Invited guests only."

"No, Pa. We've got to pay," Eleanor informed him apologetically. "They haven't any money."

Even with some diners, the new restaurant lacked atmosphere. The serviceable, heavy lunchtime tables, darkly tiled, did not look welcoming although the thick red drapes which cut off half the room added a night-time cosiness. The curtains hung on rings from a long pole balanced at either end between two loops. Thus making it easy enough to turn the Changing Scene back into the Bond Street Buffet for the morning.

"That must be the man from the *Daily Post,*" Eleanor whispered as they sat down. He was masticating a chop as Hugo, in tails, approached his table with an ingratiating smile.

"Good evening," he said.

"Good evening."

"They call me Lucky Morrow." Hugo was speaking in

rather a surprising American accent.

"I know, I saw your picture outside," the man answered, putting some carrot into his mouth.

"I suppose you've heard the one about the plastic surgeon who melted in front of the fire?" Hugo leaned over the table and appeared to pluck something from the lone diner's top pocket. He blew on his cupped fists. "Hocus pocus . . . fish bones choke us!" His fingers worked to produce a shimmering red silk handkerchief with a plaster egg inside it.

"Hey!" he exclaimed, displaying his empty hands in the air. "Thank you very much!"

The man smiled and sipped his wine.

"What about the peacock who said to his mate, 'I'm game if you are!'" A small vase stuffed with plastic flowers materialised in the air and Hugo popped it down beside the customer's glass.

"Hey, hey! Watch the birdie! A miracle a minute!"

"Ha!" said his audience, fairly genially.

At this Hobbs lost his nerve. He clicked his fingers and sang a note or two. "That 'ole black magic has me in its spell . . . ber, ber, ber . . .!" He backed from the table, swivelled indecisively, turned unsmilingly on his heel and approached the couple sitting in the corner.

"Hi there! They call me Lucky Morrow."

"Would you care to see the menu?" Toby Broadbent said to the Mackies.

Norman Mackie sighed with relief. "Ah yes . . . at last, good. Thank you."

"What a wonderful selection you've managed to prepare for your opening," Mrs Mackie smiled encouragingly at the youthful new proprietor. "I feel sure you're going to do very well with this spec."

He looked pleased. "We're hoping so."

Norman Mackie was fond of food. He also had a nervous stomach and didn't like to wait too long for it. "Now, dear, I don't know about you and Nella but I think I might settle for sole."

"No sole, I'm afraid," Broadbent said.

"No sole . . ." his wife murmured placatingly. "Never mind, there's so much else for us to choose from. I like the sound of duckling on a bed of rice, with young farm peas."

Toby Broadbent bowed low over her menu as if he might see something he didn't know himself. "Duckling's off, this evening, actually," he revealed apologetically.

"Is it . . . ah. Let me see then. Well, I think the best plan, Toby, is for you to advise us. My husband doesn't like anything with vinegar in it."

Their order taken, they sat back and waited. Hugo's voice floated across the empty room. " . . . the one about the man who got muddled between incest and arson and set fire to his sister."

Eleanor giggled. "That joke's quite funny."

"Why is he talking like an American?" Her father twisted in his seat. "I say, that chap's gone out some-where," he added wonderingly, as Toby Broadbent slipped out of the restaurant and disappeared down Bold Street. "I'm absolutely starving."

His wife glanced round warily then she made her voice very low and her lips mouthed emphatically as if for the deaf. "It doesn't do to make food the be-all and end-all."

"But I've got jaggers. This isn't free, you know, either. We're paying for it."

"You won't come to any harm. Oh, here comes Lucky Morrow. Hallo dear . . . we are enjoying our first visit to the Changing Scene."

Eleanor felt most excited and proud of him. "It's lovely.

93

I expect people will start coming as soon as they realise you're open at night."

"Nice place," her father agreed, "if only we could get something to eat."

"Toby's just slipped out for one or two things he's run out of," Hugo tweaked at his cuffs, snapped his fingers and did a few quick tap steps. He produced his cards and let the pack fly back from one hand to the other.

"Take a card, lady," he said to Mrs Mackie, strongly American and staring rather fiercely. "Wouldya look at it, please. Hearts, diamonds, clubs or spades. Commit it to memory. I ask you not to divulge your chosen card to us."

He was stunningly talented at card tricks. Eleanor sat back, knowing her parents would be impressed. He could even tell anyone which card they'd thought of without first rippling through the pack and influencing their choice.

"And now may I borrow your watch, Sir?"

Mr Mackie undid the strap and handed it to him.

Hugo wrapped it in a napkin, laid the bulging parcel on a corner of the table and touched it gently with a knife handle. "You won't object, I trust, if I smash this watch into small fragments for the purposes of my next breathtaking illusion?"

The Mackies were smiling.

"Thank you very much! Here we go!" Hugo raised the knife handle and stepped back. He trod on to Toby Broadbent who was speeding to the table with all their first course plates, cleverly balanced in the waiter's manner.

Broadbent let fly with a shower of white bait.

With an almighty crash the plates hit the tiles and went on splintering. Toby Broadbent stepped on a piece of melon, seized at the corner of the table, knocked Mr Mackie's watch off and dived into the red curtains. As the pole

94

slipped from its loop, they came down slowly and enveloped him.

"I hope this is an illusion," Eleanor's father said.

Eleanor thought she would never be able to stop laughing.

"Heaven, poor Tob . . ." Her mother was on her feet to help. "Don't say anything," she warned her husband.

" . . . not say anything?" His voice came, thin and aggrieved, into the stunned silence, "Why shouldn't I? I've got to say something if my watch has gone for a burton. Grawly Mackie wore that watch in the Boer War."

"If there's any damage, Mr Mackie," Hugo exclaimed wretchedly, "the Changing Scene will take care of it."

But of course the Changing Scene went bankrupt and the matter of the smashed watch was neglected. It came up in rows ever after. Eleanor said he hadn't bothered. She said Hugo bothered if he could and, if he couldn't, he didn't bother. He said he never had the money and in any case it was Toby Broadbent's responsibility. He said she had put her father's watch before him.

The watch episode, coinciding with Hugo's breakthrough into professional conjuring, simply brought their situation to a sour head. He went off to work in the northern clubs and she went on loving Robin Stewart White. She didn't see Hugo again until years later when his marriage to Barbara had collapsed.

"You know, I rather liked old Barbara," Marian admitted to Eleanor. They were standing in the kitchen together preparing food for her husband's sixtieth birthday party. "She wasn't nearly as bloody as Hugo made out. I know she stifled him, and he got that obsession about Mrs Pope attempting to poison him, but he gave her a rotten time, lugging her round the country, with her mopping and mowing in the back of that old van. I expect she's stifling Mart now, is she? Don't you wish that child weren't growing up in Morecambe?"

Martin was Hugo's son. That small boy who once stood beside their bed saying, 'While you slept your heads were banging together,' was now taking A levels and wanting to work in the city. She'd have liked to be there when he came to live in London. Breaking the news to him that things were not as everlasting as he'd expected seemed a bit gutless. It might not have been any different either if they'd had a child of their own.

She reached for another tomato to cut up. "You and Peter have been extremely devoted, haven't you."

Marian paused to think about it, her knife poised in the air. "Yes, I suppose we have. In our early days I was always having hysterics and locking myself in the bedroom. I'd lurk hopefully, shouting, 'Why don't you break the door down?' Peter simply fell asleep on the sofa. It took me some time to accept him like that and laugh about it and feel he did love me even if he didn't bash the bedroom door to matchwood. Talking of passion, my dear, how is your admirer?"

"No sign." She couldn't tell Marian that Hugo was having her trailed. It sounded so absurd. So alien and seedy and desperate. As if they were two black sheep outside the normal rules of social intercourse. It must mean that Hugo looked on her now as simply one more vexacious item in his life to be attacked and crushed.

Dwelling on her marriage brought her to the conclusion that her own existence was at its lowest ebb ever. All props were disappearing at once. Eric Clover had forced his friendship on her under false pretences and she'd fallen for

96

it like a pathetic old bag, hoping to rekindle the romance of youth and find some comfort. She wasn't going to speak to him, or about him, ever again. How ironical that such a dismissable young man had been able to make fools of them both with such ease. Making a supreme effort to keep calm, she changed the subject and tried to work herself into a more positive and buoyant mood for Marian's sake and her own.

It was a warm night and the party was as pleasant as she'd expected it to be. Summer Corner, Marian and Peter's house, looked out over the Estuary marshes. As the sun set, the Welsh coast stood out in breath-catching clarity on the other side of the water.

Guests took their drinks and wandered out into the garden. A few of the braver ones had a quick dip in the homemade pool. Eleanor picked up a tray of caviar toasties and started to make the rounds. She was greeting people she'd known her entire life. She'd known their parents. Her parents had known their grandparents. In middle age, mysteriously, that began to matter. Through them, perhaps, she held on to her father. And now, to Uncle Hunt.

"Hallo John."

"Nella!" A tall, gently stooping six foot three, the man put down his glass in order to hug her. "How lovely to see you!"

In her mother's photograph drawer, there was a snap of herself and John Rush (a recently nominated Conservative candidate), sharing a pram on holiday when they were both a few weeks old. Nanny Rush, with darkly enigmatic smile, was bowling them along, beside Criccieth Castle, to the shore. The fathers would have been playing golf, Jack Rush, a lay preacher, threatening to quit the course if her father used any more foul language when he missed a shot.

Across the rockery was Sue Morrison, JP, beaming away at fourteen stone in blue silk, who was in the sandpit on Eleanor's first day at school. Busily occupied that kindergarten morning making sandpies, she'd gone on steadily through life in the same steadfast manner. Unmarried still, she wore rings on her wedding finger. A bride of public service.

Ian Kemp was at the party. He'd threatened to cut off her nose and kill her with a dolly peg. While she awaited death at his hands, she had sleepless nights. She was going to remind him of their brief moment of kindergarten glory as the Prince and Princess.

When the parents came by invitation to school to see how their children were progressing, Ian Kemp and Eleanor Mackie were chosen as prince and princess for a performance of singing and dancing. She remembered those parents, mostly mothers on the weekday morning, sitting obediently in rows on tiny children's chairs. Her own mother was alert and straight-backed and faintly smiling which meant she was braced for catastrophe. That was the face she'd worn later at gymkhanas.

Eleanor had to stand in the middle while the other children danced round her in a circle, singing to Miss Nightingale at the piano and the accompanying thunder of twenty pairs of Clarks' sandals. 'The princess was a lovely child, a lovely child, a lovely child.' For the next verse they stretched up their arms and turned into trees. They pressed in upon the princess to show time was passing and the forest growing tall and thick. 'She fell asleep for a hundred years, a hundred years, a hundred years.'

"Yes, we don't get to London as much as we'd like to, what with the children's school situation, and one thing and another," Ian Kemp was saying. His once-jolly eyes

98

had gone dead, she noticed. His wife, Vivien Fairchild, was still calling herself by her maiden name although she had done nothing except be his wife.

Didn't Ian remember being the handsome prince who came 'galloping by, galloping by, galloping by'? He'd smashed through the trees to rescue her and she'd danced with him in her red kilt, faster and faster. He was bald now, and redundant, with a caviar toastie crumb stuck to his double chin.

"What are you drinking, Nella?" Marian's husband, Peter, filled her glass. "How's Hunt?"

"In a bad way. It's such a bleak existence for him."

"I must try and pop in for a few minutes sometime."

But he never would, she knew, and she didn't blame him. By the time Peter got to know Huntly Quinton, her uncle had already lost his money and he wasn't bothering to be sociable any more.

As it grew dark, Eleanor lit a cigarette to keep the midges away. All the smoking going on added a piratical dash to the party atmosphere as if this agreeable northern garden was a last bastion of red-bloodedness where men were still men and thought nothing of the morrow. In fact, they did think of the morrow. More probably, than her friends in London did, but they didn't speak of it. These genial unpredatory men steered clear of serious subjects and stuck, in the old-fashioned manner, to things which didn't matter. Possibly, Eleanor decided, it had to do with keeping up a front in a community, with their businesses, their governorships and their committees. Their existences had been handed down to them so they weren't conceited or censorious or competitive. Those were London characteristics, where the rats rise to the top and the rich are property advisers, money dealers and public relations consultants. Here, they were complacent. Not snobbish necessarily, just class conscious. Old Them and Us attitudes still existed. Thems in her youth were heroes like Jellicoe of Jutland or towering figures like Lloyd George and F E Smith, names on every father's lips. Us were the Mackies, the Hobbs, the Rushes and the Kemps. The Us camp knew their place too and were pleased with it.

Snippets of conversation floated across the evening air.

"It's not very pleasant, is it, to have a brother who goes old-tyme dancing in a gay ballroom in Southport?"

"I don't care for ballet either. I've always assumed it was just an excuse for them to jump on each other."

She turned, stiff-faced, when she thought she heard a familiar laugh but it wasn't Robin. She'd been watching and listening all evening, hoping he might suddenly walk in. Absurd to hope. Marian wouldn't have dreamed of inviting them both to the same gathering.

"All right, they have their so-called democratic meetings but woe betide anybody who speaks out against council policy. They're given a rough ride with some very bad behaviour."

"It's all very well, but you can't leave people without hope. You don't have to throw money at them, and walk off, but you've got to create a climate in which they can start to help themselves. This economy is too harsh for Liverpool. Encouragement and incentives are needed."

"What it amounts to is a generation's been sacrificed which would have sacrificed us. The Waynes and Grants and Lees of this world are natural pawns to be used by people like Scargill."

Later on, Peter sat down beside Eleanor. "I saw your friend Robin Stewart White a little while ago."

"Oh, did you?" Something skipped inside her. "I haven't seen him for years. Is he back here?"

"Told me he lives in Wiltshire. Never married! All your fault, poor chap. You obviously blighted his life, Nella!"

"It isn't true," she said, laughing.

"Well, he says he has a housekeeper. I got the impression he only comes up occasionally. Their offices were taken over, you know, in Liverpool, but I gather he still goes round the world although the markets have all changed."

Marian called to him, "Darling, give me a hand with these plates, will you."

Eleanor watched them standing together. In a deceptive patch of light from the windows, they seemed to be growing alike. She envied them the dependable presence they presented in the district. At sixty, Peter still insisted on eating rice and potato on the same plate. Adventurousness in eating nearly always boded badly. There was a lot to be said for the rice and potato men.

She was talking to Jeremy, the youngest of their four boys, when Peter's sister, Priscilla, came up and joined them.

"Hugo not with you?"

"Got a lot on at the moment," she replied, as she'd had to do all the years of their marriage. Hugo had never felt he belonged in the way she had but then his mother had grown up in Ireland and he'd been sent away to Switzerland for school.

"Marian looks super, don't you think?" Priscilla had been on a diet and her head seemed enormous, like a three month foetus.

"Yes she does."

"Did you see she's wearing Mother's diamond necklace?"

"How wonderful!"

"Yes, it is wonderful." Priscilla gave a rather common sniffing twitch which drew her mouth up at one side, "They were Grandmother Porter's diamonds."

"They're very nice."

"Well, I can't deny Marian does a lot for Mother. She's for ever trekking over to Freshfield to help her, so I suppose it's only right for her to have Mother's diamonds."

"Your mother will want the grandchildren to have them eventually, won't she."

"I don't know what Mother wants, frankly. She gave me her emerald ring, you know. When my daughter, Lucinda, borrowed it for the evening, Mother took one look at it and then asked for it back. So now I've lost it."

"Ah. But you'll get it back."

"Will I? D'you think I will? D'you hear that, Peter? Nella says I'm to have Mother's ring back. Don't you, Nella?"

Peter's response was mercifully lost as the burglar alarm went off in the next-door house. Marian ran to ring the police but otherwise nobody took much notice.

"I'll come with you," Eleanor said.

"It'll be another false alarm. What a bore. That burglar alarm of the Hutchings is becoming a bloody nuisance." She rooted in a basket of fruit and found the keys. "They'll be in Spain for another month."

Police cars were speeding down the road as they turned into the Hutchings' drive.

In the darkness a couple of policemen disappeared under the trees round the side of the house. Two more met Marian and Eleanor on the doorstep.

Marian greeted them with an apologetic smile. "Thanks awfully for coming. This is becoming rather a habit but I have to take precautions since it's not my house. I've got the keys." She opened the front door and stood back.

"After you, madam," said the officer.

She laughed. "Not bloody likely!" she said, drink making her theatrically matey. "After you, *mes enfants*!"

The two women waited in the hall while the policemen searched the house. Marian slumped on a chair, idly turning the pages of a copy of *Country Life* which was lying on the chest. They could hear the walkie talkies moving round upstairs.

"Oh, Nella . . . sorry." Marian sighed, shook her head and raised her eyes to the ceiling. "This is the second time it's happened, you know. I can't imagine what sets the alarm off. They won't find anything."

The police found the three burglars hiding in a back bedroom. In a towel on the bed there was jewellery, some bits of silver and a carriage clock.

It was two youths and a girl. As the thieves were escorted downstairs, Marian stood up and moved towards the staircase. Eleanor saw her sway with shock.

"Emma!"

The girl never looked at them. She went past, straight-backed, staring defiantly ahead.

"You know her?"

"That's Ian Kemp's daughter," Marian said.

"Drugs?"

She nodded. "My God. Poor old Ian. They've had such a time with it."

Eleanor said nothing. She was stunned too. So the Prince's life wasn't all that happy ever after, after all.

Chapter 6

Three days later, Eleanor saw Eric Clover waiting in the hospital car park. She felt a positive thrill of hatred at his cheek.

Without glancing at him, she locked the car door and strode straight down the path towards the geriatric wards.

"Wait for me!" he called.

She turned. "Just get lost, will you. I don't ever want to see you again."

"Let me . . ."

"Don't come any further, for God's sake. Don't you dare besmirch my uncle's illness with your cheating scumlike presence. I will kill you if you go anywhere near him."

He stepped after her inside the sliding doors.

"Get out of here!"

He hesitated as if deciding whether to stop her by force. He started to follow her down the empty corridor then stopped to tie a flapping shoe lace.

She couldn't stop. She was beside herself with fury. She saw a trolley, laden with bedpans, and she gripped it, whirled it into position and sent it winging into his crouching form. The bedpans bounced away on the linoleum as she skipped grimly round the corner into the commanding form of Sister Packer.

"Sister, I'm afraid there's a man throwing your bedpans about. He looks to me as if he's from the psychiatric wards." Eleanor passed on to find her uncle.

"Hallo, Uncle Hunt."

He was sitting beside his bed in his chair. His head was hanging. She didn't know whether he was asleep or in despair. The sight of him, so grey, so thin, so gormless, stopped her breath.

"Uncle Hunt?"

He woke and smiled and reached out for her.

It was a bad day for him, she could tell. He was shifting about in pain.

She sat there, her hands shaking, trying to calm herself.

"You know, Nella, I'd like to hear a little more about the crash that put me in here? I'm pretty certain I wasn't drinking at the time? I'd cut that right out." His hand sliced the air emphatically. "Phut!"

"There wasn't a crash. You had a clot in your leg, that's what it was. Still, you're getting on fine now. Ma is tremendously pleased to be hearing such good reports about you."

"How is Ma? I've been thinking about Ma and Pam recently. I've been sitting here thinking about what's happened and a lot of other things. Frankly, sweet, I really feel I'm more reasonable now than at any time in my life."

"Yes, each experience has a value, I'm certain. Well, you've come to a splendid place."

"Very true. I saw an advertisement in the paper, sent them a note and here I am."

There was a sudden flurry from the bed in the corner. "Nurse! Nurse!" Mr Eastwood called, "Have you brought me the Scotch I ordered?"

"That cakey cow wants some cheap whisky. I think he's after one of the waitresses here."

"I'll enquire about it, Mr Eastwood," Eleanor told him. "How about a piece of chocolate in the meantime?"

"Thank you so much."

As he ate a finger of Kit Kat, a stream of brown spittle dribbled down his chin. She wiped it away with a tissue, holding her breath.

"When the weather's warmer, we'll be able to go for a drive," she suggested to her uncle. "We might go to Parkgate and have a picnic."

"I'd like that."

"Ma was saying New Zealand is most beautiful."

He nodded dreamily. "I've heard that, Nella," he said, and then there was a lengthy silence.

'How can I stay long?' she was thinking, 'I can't stand it.'

"Nurse! Nurse!" shouted Mr Eastwood.

Her mind was filled with Eric Clover. She was in a turmoil. Because of men, women seemed to spend the first half of their lives wishing to kill themselves and the second half wishing to commit homicide.

Hunt's head drooped again and his eyes closed.

"What did you do today?"

"Mm . . . ?"

"What did you do today?"

"Very little, sweet. They asked me to help them out in the hospital bar, owing to my previous experience as a publican."

For a moment she believed it. Believed there was a hospital bar. She was becoming as batty as anybody herself. Poor Uncle Hunt. His awful pub in Harlech had been a riot. He was roaring drunk behind the bar, menacing the customers and telling them to sod off.

Dwelling on his black times naturally depressed him but talk of his distant past amused him and cheered him up. She could tell he was pondering on that as the days crawled by with nothing in them but memories. Nearly everything to do with the Liverpool Huntly Quinton belonged to was gone.

"They were an elegant crowd on the Cotton Market, you know . . . race horses and that sort of thing. Some of them were very wealthy. Queen Victoria said they were the best dressed men in the country. Certainly, if you wanted to cut any ice, you had to start on your own. Everybody else was paid in washers."

Eleanor passed him a peppermint, relieved to have got him talking. "Did they all get illnesses from working with cotton?" She was going to confront Hugo with this detective business. What a blasted idiot he was.

"Everybody's lungs got damaged. You couldn't help it. It wasn't bad though. People only coughed occasionally. I never heard anyone complain about being unduly affected. You got used to it."

"Were there troubles then?" Hugo was a bastard. Eric Clover was a bastard. She was on her own, that was the truth . . . like Uncle Hunt.

"Ooh yes, those Liverpool Irish! They were shockers. Damnable. If you could control them, you were really something. Of course, they worked for nothing in the past and they don't forget it now."

"Pa told me people never stayed in Liverpool. Is that right? They came here, he said, from other places and then moved on to settle somewhere else?"

That broke the spell. Hunt looked up and beamed affectionately. "What's Norming doing today?" he asked. "Has he gone to golf?"

Golf. Oh God. He couldn't play golf for ages before he died.

She smiled too. "He's watching television, I expect," she answered gently, then she stood up and tucked his blanket in, in case she cried. "I must slip away now. Hugo's going to ring me."

"Robin looked in yesterday after you departed," Uncle Hunt declared, as she was stocking sweets and cigarettes into his bedside drawer. "He told me he'd glimpsed Hugo's sister, Marian, in some shop or other."

"What was Robin doing here?"

"Mm . . . what's that, sweet?"

"What . . . is . . . Robin . . . doing . . . here?"

"I think he likes to keep an eye on me, you know. I'm surprised you missed him."

God in heaven. His mind had completely gone. Robin Stewart White would not be coming within two hundred miles of this geriatric cesspit.

When she reached home, Eric Clover was waiting outside the house. She was too depressed to argue. She let him in.

She sat slumped opposite him in a chair. Her head always seemed to be aching these days. "But you betrayed me and you've betrayed my husband," she said, draining her third whisky.

She'd always known one tampered at one's peril with these odd little weasels one didn't really want. In the end they had an uncanny power to undermine and deal out rejection. The inferior mostly rejects the superior.

A desire to fly across the room and kick him was overwhelming her. Only age, and the big windows, back and front, turning the house into a goldfish bowl, stopped her. What an awful idiot he was. She'd taught him how to look aloof and confident and now the gauche oaf was looking it in that ridiculous designer jacket.

She tried to keep her voice down and not scandalise her mother's neighbours. "Don't you ever dare attempt to go near my uncle in that hospital. D'you understand? I adore him. I'm not having him caught up in this unsavoury rubbish. You keep away . . . or I . . . well, I'm reporting you for harassment. You'll get an injunction served on you."

She got up. On her way out of the room she landed him a swift sly kick which could have been an accident. "He's dying, you fool. God Almighty. He is dying, with his leg cut off. You're such a cheating little swine. I want you out of this house."

She could hear him swear under his breath.

"Go now, for goodness' sake."

Clutching his leg, he limped out after her into the hall. She was holding the front door wide open for him to go.

"If I go, that's it. I'm not ever coming here again."

"That's what I want."

"You're a bitch, you know that. Hugo must think you are and he's right."

Eleanor wanted to burst with rage. She spoke very slowly, her teeth bared like a dog, to make him see what he'd done.

"You made friends with me under false pretences. You wasted my time asking and asking questions about me, about Hugo, and everything to do with my life. It wasn't for friendship, that's what's so awful about it, it was . . ."

"Nella, listen, I wanted . . ."

"You lied. You betrayed me and you betrayed . . ."

"I like you, you silly woman. I didn't have to get to know you. Can't you see that? I could have gone on following you and you'd never have been any the wiser. Would you?"

She said nothing.

"I wanted you to find my notes about you. I didn't see how I was going to tell you." In his face now she saw everything. Response, perception, vulnerability. Was it true? Was it? "Come on. That's the honest truth, I promise you."

She stayed, uncertain, her hand on the door, knowing it might be true. She couldn't abide him and she couldn't bear him to go. She was upset. But exhilarated.

He watched her hesitation. She saw his expression harden. She no longer knew whether she'd taught him or whether he'd always known better. He moved forward to close the front door.

He pushed her back against it. He held her there as he kissed her. His other hand hoiked up her skirt.

"I don't want a parcel of Aids, thanks."

"Bit late to think about that now." He laughed so softly, it might not have been a laugh at all. "If I go, you'll be coming with me."

In the kitchen the telephone started ringing. He tightened his hold so she couldn't escape to answer it. "Leave it. It'll be Hugo. Here endeth my reports!"

She pulled free. "It could be the hospital. Don't you worry your head about those reports." Giving him a grim little smile over her shoulder, she went to answer the telephone. "I'll be writing those myself from now on."

It wasn't Hugo. It was a call from one of her mother's poetry friends, Miss Thorogood, asking after Uncle Hunt.

As she jotted down the message on a convenient piece of cardboard, an idea for an early revenge occurred to her.

Later on, after Eric had gone, she collected some bits and

pieces from round the house then, laughing to herself, she sat down at the dining room table with a small box. Inside it, on a base of black cardboard, she glued some fronds of maidenhair fern. Criss-crossed chicken bones were carefully laid in place on top of that and on a plain white card in capital letters she printed BREATHE YOUR LAST! She had a look in her diary for a suitable date and added SATURDAY, 4 AUGUST, which was some way off. In the morning she'd post the parcel to someone in London to post on to Hugo. If he wanted to play games, he'd come to the right person.

She was pleased when Eric reappeared the next day. She was weeding the garden, wondering where he was and hoping he'd come.

"I'll take you out to dinner," he said, splaying himself across the garden seat and patting his wallet pocket to see that his money was there.

"No need for that," she answered, "I don't want anybody gawping at us. We'd better have supper here."

So they began again. Eleanor did wonder, in all the circumstances, what she was doing. She didn't approve of what he'd done and she didn't approve of herself. But then she didn't approve of Hugo either. Just a bit longer, she'd decide when she was calm. When she got worked up she frequently told Eric Clover to leave her alone there and then, and worried in case he did. The excitement muted the depression of the visits to Uncle Hunt. It buoyed her up because the meetings had an urgency. Whether it was the wondrous sexual excitement at her age or knowing they wouldn't have long together, she wasn't certain. Musing on that, she started to watch him. 'I could tell him not to say horse riding and par*don*. It could be all right.'

Word had spread that she was back in the district and old friends started to get in touch. She put them off, making Hunt her excuse.

She was writing reports about herself for Hugo.

She usually did them in an old exercise book, sitting up in bed beside Eric Clover while they watched television on a small black and white set perched on the chest of drawers.

Our subject she called herself at first. No, no, not subject. That didn't sound right. She crossed it out and turned over to a new page. What was private eye vernacular? "Mrs X rose early this morning," she remarked out loud in a chatty manner as she wrote it down.

"I can't hear the television if you're going to talk," Eric said.

"D'you call me Mrs X?"

"E."

"Familiar from the start. How often d'you do it?"

He shifted restlessly. "Come on, I can't concentrate. Once a week . . . all right? You never go anywhere so there's nothing to say. And Hugo's getting a bit sheepish about it."

"Sheepish, is he? Good. Well, E will be doing a bit more from now on. You should be sheepish too."

His eyes stayed on the television but she could see his mouth going up at the corner. "Not my style, sheepish."

"Am I the oldest woman you've ever known?"

"Yes."

"In that case go down and get me a banana, will you. Your legs are younger than mine."

"I'll go when I get up to clean my teeth."

10 a.m. — left for Liverpool. Following at a discreet

distance, I kept her under constant surveillance. "How do you spell surveillance?"

"Not a word I'd use."

Proceeding at a discreet distance, I ascertained E made no assignation. Her destination turned out to be sundry shops of an expensive nature, where she tried on coats, jackets and skirts. Posing as an arrestingly lifelike model of the man about town, I noted no price tag less than three figures. E bought two skirts, two jackets and a blue silk handkerchief (possibly for your good self). After a light lunch at Dubby's Wine Bar in Albert Dock, she purchased a black and white silk dress costing £595.99. and took a taxi home — a distance of some sixteen miles. "What's Albert Dock like?"

"It's brilliant. I'll take you there."

E remained at home until 2000 hours when she emerged from the house in black and white silk (looking stunning), and got into her car. She drove straight to an imposing pink residence called The Beeches . . . "No, not The Beeches," she mused, "I want something more like Dunshoppin . . . er . . . yes . . . Dovelands." . . . *Dovelands, Parkhouse Drive. Concealing myself discreetly behind a tree, I peered through a crack in the curtains at the assembled gathering. All were naked. Middle-aged gentlemen, handicapped by abdominal ballooning and the limp dick syndrome, pranced round with grapes etc. E, like other ladies present, wore only a necklace and gold party sandals for the money-no-object champagne buffet supper. With the aid of advanced electronic equipment, I ascertained the subjects of conversation at this wife swapping orgy: washing machines and golf.*

"What's all this rot?" Eric took the exercise book from

her and read what she had written. *E disappeared into an opulently appointed bedroom with a randy stud* he wrote across the bottom in his flowing hand. "I would never use all that archaic jargon." He switched off the television, went downstairs for her banana and then into the bathroom to get ready for bed.

Eleanor lay smiling to herself, waiting for him to come.

He came at a scamper, in his pale blue T-shirt and whirled under the duvet. Icy hands reached out for her as she put the light out. She gave little shrieks.

"Don't put the light off."

"Got to."

"But I want to see you."

"I'm too fat."

"Does Hugo do this to you?"

"You mustn't do it."

"Sometimes old matrons taste very pungent. I like it. Am I the best ever?"

"Very nearly."

"Who's the best?"

"Don't!" She wriggled away from him.

"Come on, who was the best? I know who it is. It's Robin Stewart White, isn't it?"

She felt a stab of shock. "So that's it! Hugo told you to look out for him, did he?"

"I know all about it," he said but he went on asking questions.

Later, in the dark, when she was half asleep, he spoke again. "Does Hugo know Dr Gurbuz?"

"Dr Kolicassides."

"Kolicassides? Of Turkey?"

"No, Holloway Road," she murmured dreamily. "He's never been to Turkey."

"I shouldn't be too sure of that."

"I am sure." She sat up. "Eric, we go to Dr Baldwin in York Street. What's the matter? Are you ill?"

He laughed and pulled her down. "Who's this Kolicassides then?" He held her hand and pressed his fingers determinedly through hers.

Her eyes closed again. "Well, nothing. He's a doctor in Holloway. Hugo hates him. He leaves messages in Greek on the answerphone. That's why we go to Dr Baldwin. Tell me the Girl Guide story again."

"I'm too tired."

"Go on."

"Once upon a time," he began, terribly quietly, "there was a naughtly little Girl Guide. She was in the Imp Patrol and, just like you when you were asked to leave the Girl Guides, she hated being sent off to collect wood for the camp fire. This time she wandered off by herself, muttering rude words and she was lost in the grounds of an old monastery where she fell into the hands of the cruel abbot. He ordered her to kneel down. She was undressed before him and tied to the altar."

Eleanor smiled in the darkness inside his arm. "Then what?" Her hand moved down to touch him.

Eric Clover pinned her arms behind her head. "Now you will have to be punished," the abbot said to her.

When there were only three days to go before the fourth of August, Hugo finally reacted to Eleanor's parcel of chicken bones and fern warning him to breathe his last.

"Look," he said, most casually, over the telephone, "is it wise to have this sort of lengthy separation? I have a feeling it isn't really. Why don't I come up there for a day or two? I'd like to see Hunt anyway and Bad Dog would enjoy some shore walks."

She pressed her mouth against the back of her hand lest she laughed out loud. "What a good . . ." In the bathroom above her head Eric Clover broke into a sort of sea shanty. Paralysed, she jumped to shut the kitchen door. "What a good idea."

"What's the matter?"

"Nothing."

"This Friday I thought might be most suit . . ."

"Oh dear," she interrupted quickly, "no."

"Why not?"

"I've got a dress-making appointment in London. You've just reminded me."

"You'll have to cancel it."

"I can't possibly cancel it. I won't get another appointment for ages. I'll have to come to you."

"Nella, this is ridiculous. Leave it."

She managed to persuade him that she must come and when she put the telephone down again, she felt a great relief. However daunting the confrontation, it was high time she and Hugo put a stop to all this deceit. She set out two days later planning to stay for the weekend.

The Liverpool train was a little late at Euston and, as usual, it went without saying, so was Hugo. There was no sign of him. Passengers from the train loped their way down the platform with their luggage to where husbands, wives, grandmothers or children waited beyond the barrier in an expectant punctual clutch, their faces brightening in turn. No face brightened for her. Her own face set like a trap. Suddenly, intensely weary, she put her bag down and prepared to wait.

Ten minutes later, he appeared, looking Eleanor noted,

meek as a blasted mouse. "Ah, here already! Sorry about that. You're just in, I suppose?"

"No."

He kissed her. "I was caught by that new woman in Abigail Road."

Hugo had one or two spots. He didn't look well.

"What's the news?" she asked, as they drove away from the station towards home.

"Nothing much," he replied casually, "I've had a death threat."

"Heavens." She glanced at him, caught the aura of injured innocence and had to stare ahead, clenching her teeth, in case she laughed and laughed. "*Death threat?*"

"It's only some camp joke," he assured her in a bored, disgusted voice. He overtook two cars and narrowly missed a lorry coming in the opposite direction. "Some arsehole put bones in a box of greenery and there was a note in yobbish writing telling me to breathe my last. Bad Dog got hold of the box and made short work of that. Actually, I've narrowed it down to those gay builders in Edgar's garden. They've been behaving very annoyingly. George's father is dying to have a go at them."

"Not with his van wing I hope."

"I might give him twenty quid to swish past their windpipes."

"Good God, Hugo, you mustn't do anything like that."

He turned right round in his seat, as if to confirm the depth of her reaction, and laughed. "That leathery woman is stirring up a lot of trouble in the road."

"How d'you mean?"

"She's making a nuisance of herself. I knew she would."

"How?"

"Well, she's into everything, isn't she. She was doing her grotesquely battling best to persuade me to sign a petition against somebody's barking dog. But she's always out there, looking very intense and white in the face, complaining and ferreting things out."

"How awful. What does she think she's doing?"

"I've told you, she's trying to get as close as she can to the heartbeat of anarchy."

"What's her job?"

"Some sort of careers adviser apparently. Yesterday, I asked her if she ever said to anyone, 'Well, you are crassly stupid, thick-skinned, devious and lazy, you'd better be a builder,' but she was not amused. There was a photograph of her, with her wet wimp of a designer husband, badger bald, having one of those richly rewarding lunches of their choice in the pages of the colour supplement.

"She also has an appalling child," he added, speaking in a kind of humorous roar to emphasise the appallingness. "It's stoney-eyed, surly . . . it's *shocking*! It radiates rudeness. When it fixes you with its silent gaze, you want to hold up a crucifix to drive the evil back!" He threw back his head, making a horrified gargling noise in his throat. "Ah, we've had it, I'm afraid," he dropped his voice as they drew up outside the house. "Here they are."

A thin woman was wheeling a push chair with a child walking beside it.

"This is my wife," Hugo said, "I don't believe we . . ."

"Hi! Kiki Day," she replied briskly, holding out her hand and putting her head on one side to give Eleanor an unsmiling scrutiny.

Eleanor asked her how she was enjoying Abigail Road.

As they exchanged a few words of conversation, Mr Sharkey's door opened and the old man came out. His plastic mac was tied with string round the middle and one huge foot was padded and bound up in a plastic bag. He was carrying a bucket.

"There goes Mr Sharkey. He is such a dear!" Kiki Day remarked approvingly, smiling first at him then down at her stone-eyed Antichrist. "Louise adores him. One of the best features of Abigail Road as far as we're concerned. He's been here for yonks, I gather. Wave to Mr Sharkey, darling." Mother and daughter waved.

The filthy old man squinted malevolently up and down the road then he scuttled out into the gutter and sloshed the contents of the bucket outside her house.

"He looks a mess but he's so independent. We think he's wonderful," Kiki Day continued in her thin voice. "He does everything for himself because he's determined to go on being his own person. I don't know if you've noticed how he brings out his own little newspaper packets of rubbish for the litter bins."

"Little packets of excrement, I'm afraid," Hugo told her.

"*Excrement?*" she looked stern as if she couldn't quite believe what a bad joke she'd heard.

The Hobbs nodded.

"But what's Abigail Road doing about it?" she snapped. "He should be in care."

Their conversation was interrupted as a figure with black homburg, blue Mothercare coat and briefcase, hastened up the steps of their house and rang the bell.

Bad Dog barked. Eleanor's chest lurched with apprehension as Hugo broke away to see who it was.

"Can I help you?"

"Here I am again, Mr Hobbs!"

"Yes?"

"I've come to see you."

"Well, yes. But who on earth are you?"

"It's Mr Majid, with special reference to your council grant outstanding."

"Mr Majid! How nice to see you. I didn't recognise you. I must say you're looking quite different."

Mr Majid buckled over with a gust of delighted laughter. "Not looking so devilishly like our friend, Mr Michael Caine, today!"

Hugo and Eleanor were equally convulsed.

"Do come in," Hugo said, "I think you'll be quite pleasantly surprised." He opened the front door, stepped inside to hold on to the dog, and put his keys down on the hall chest. "Hey, no, just one minute, Mr Majid." He pulled the door to and came outside again, "I want to show you all the new work we've done by the basement door."

Kiki Day didn't go away. "Is Mr Majid from the Council?" she demanded, staring curiously. "What department is it? We're going to have to do something collectively about that old man."

Unnoticed by the adults, the Day child slipped up the steps into the Hobbs' house. The front door slammed. Bad Dog greeted it with a roar and the child let out an ear-splitting scream.

Kiki Day, the Hobbs and Mr Majid all ran up the steps to the front door. There was utter confusion.

"There's no need to panic," Hugo said, "Eleanor has a key."

She rooted in her bag but, for once, probably because of her disturbed state, she couldn't find it. "Wait a minute, Baddie. Be a good boy . . . I'm coming!"

Hearing her voice, the dog went mad with excitement.

Kiki Day's disapproval radiated over them. "Personally,

I'd never keep a dog unless I lived in the country. It's not fair to them."

Tight-lipped, Eleanor seized a briefcase sitting on the step beside her. Assuming it was her husband's, she whipped it open and turned it upside down. She shook the contents on to the front step.

"*Mrs Hobbs!*"

As the alien papers showered about their feet, she realised she'd never seen the briefcase in her life. It belonged to Mr Majid.

Her eyes closed with giddiness as she tried to focus on him.

"Mr Majid . . . oh how terrible! Can you ever forgive me?" Drops of sweat fell from her forehead as she stuffed the confidential pages back into their case. "I thought it was my husband's briefcase."

Hugo looked every bit as shocked as Mr Majid. His head was on one side. His expression one of total disbelief.

He crouched down to the letter box and spoke through it. The tip of Bad Dog's long sniffing Afghan nose was almost touching his.

"Now . . . er, Louise? Louise, *isn't it*? Hallo there! This is Mr Hobbs speaking! *You* are all right, aren't you? Bad Dog is a *very good dog* really and *he* won't hurt *you*. Mummy wants you to go into that room beside you and bring a hard chair to the door. When you've got the chair, Mummy says to climb on to it and open the front door for us. Can you do that?"

There was a silence then a terrible wail and some more roaring from the dog. The noise was deafening.

"Is he biting her?" the mother demanded grimly.

"He bit me," said Mr Majid, "I'll never forget it."

Mrs Day bent down and crooned sharply under the letter box flap. "Mama's here, Loulie. Very very soon we're going to go and buy you a super King Cone because you're being such a good girl." Bad Dog hurled himself at the door with a frenzied thumping. "That poor beast is wildly frustrated."

"He's defending the house," Hugo told her shortly.

"I think we'll have to go next door," Eleanor suggested, her stomach churning. "Hugo, ask them if you can go through their house and climb over the garden wall. I'll see if Edgar's in but I don't suppose he will be."

"No, the poof's at the shop."

Mr Majid smiled at Mrs Day but his words were sharp. "We are all repenting, madam, that your child was not under supervision."

Eleanor walked with Hugo the few steps to the next house in order to swallow two milk of magnesia tablets. "My God . . . what a disaster," she murmured, under her breath.

He was fuming. "Oh shit! *Shit*. Fuck 'em!"

"Shh . . . they can hear you."

"Bastards!"

The door opened a little way and a black face appeared silently in the space. Underneath it were two or three smaller faces, ranged in size.

"Good afternoon," Hugo began politely, in a special light voice. "As you may know, we live next door and I'm afraid we've just got locked out. I wonder if I might nip into your house and hop over our garden wall?"

The faces of the new council tenants surveyed him in silence for a few seconds then there was a low suspicious murmuring from behind. "Noh, noh, noh." The door closed again.

"I'll get the police," said Kiki Day.

"Tricky, tricky!" Majid exclaimed in an excited official voice. "A grievously tricky neighbourly situation. Where the devil does the law lie here?"

"The law doesn't come into it, Mr Majid," Hugo said.

Kiki Day gasped. "You don't care if that dog savages an innocent little child?"

"Mrs Day, our builder is on the roof. I will get him to smash the attic window and rescue your child who has locked us all out of the house." He closed his eyes and pressed his fingers into his forehead then he shouted up five floors to Dave.

A piece of guttering clattered down before the face of the builder peered over.

Hobbs asked him to break into the attic and come down to open the front door.

"Will your dog bite the builder, Mr Hobbs?" Mr Majid didn't wait for an answer, "I fear this gent will be bitten. I was bitten. I'll never forget it."

On his way downstairs from the attic, brandishing a ball-claw hammer, the builder was bitten by Bad Dog and had to be taken to hospital.

"I'd like to bring back the gallows just for that builder," Hugo said, when he eventually returned from the Royal Free.

"How is Dave?" Eleanor enquired anxiously. "Is he all right?"

"He's all right," he replied, with utter gloom. "The doctor didn't seem at all worried about him but you can just imagine the song and dance we'll get from Dave now about that bitten leg. He'll be off work for *weeks and weeks and weeks.* When he does turn up, limping and whining, I will have to collect him and take him home in the evening. I'll have Majid and the People's Republic right on my back again. We are never ever going to get the work on this house finished. We've had it. That's what it amounts to." In a dreadful mood, he went to the top of the house to board up the broken attic window and remained upstairs.

Eleanor sat, stunned, then with an effort she got up.

Her throat ached. She was trying not to cry. The next thing, she knew with unswerving certainty, was that Dave would sue them.

From her cursory inspection of the house she could tell that Hugo had made a big effort for her home-coming. A casserole was simmering in the oven and he had taken the trouble to go out and find her potted shrimps to start with. Apart from his golf clubs, criss-crossed over all the armchairs to foil Bad Dog, she could see he'd done his best to tidy things up. As long as she didn't have to sit beside that hole in the sitting room wall, she would simply have to try and forget how ghastly everything was.

It seemed crass to launch into any unpleasantness over Hugo's thoughtfully prepared stew. They were both depressed and events had soared out of control. She hadn't foreseen, when she went to look after Uncle Hunt, that it was going to lead them to the brink of parting. Until now, when it was probably about to happen, she had never seriously confronted the idea of losing Hugo altogether.

They sat on at the table in the kitchen. When they were having coffee, she started hesitantly.

"I didn't want a conversation on the telephone. One half says things and they get distorted, but we'd better talk about things now. Hadn't we?"

He poured the remains of the wine into their glasses then he looked up, "What things?"

"You know what I mean. This is your fault . . . well, maybe not. Anyway, we've got to decide what we're going to do. We'll have to see whether there's any hope for us . . . I mean I don't know that there can be any in all the circumstances. I suppose we should sell this house."

"Oh come on, darling. I don't want to get into that sort of conversation at this time of night."

"You'll have to. You put us in this state."

He held out his hand in front of him and appeared to study the nails. His way of shutting off and playing for time. "Why not leave things as they are?"

She went on, carefully. "Yes, but there are many things about our state . . . well, I can't cope with them. Probably you can't. Don't you feel we should try and unravel what's happened to us?"

There was a silence. He stared at the back of his hand. "I don't see that it would be particularly helpful."

"Why not?"

"I don't think you have too bad a time with me . . . all in all." He stood up to pour more coffee then he wandered over to pick up one of his golf clubs from a chair and started to practise putting strokes.

She sat watching him, waiting. A numbness came, a kind of calm, as it does in the moment before a car crash, but he went on tapping at his ball and not saying anything.

"I know it's useless hoping to push somebody into responses they can't possibly make," she said, suddenly filled with fury, "but I don't agree with you that one should hold on to an old habit at all costs. Anyway, why are you speaking to me with all this careful casualness? What in God's name is the meaning of this private investigator you've hired? How dare you do such a thing?"

Hugo spun round, as if he'd been waiting. "Ah. So he's

made himself known to you, has he?" He flopped down into one of the armchairs in the other half of the room, which was unlit.

"You must know what's going on. You've been receiving his reports."

"I rather got the impression you were writing those yourself."

She fondled Bad Dog's ears, aware of an increasingly unreal atmosphere in the room.

She waited, too annoyed to admit anything and put herself in the wrong.

"I ought to tell you something," he went on, somewhat apologetically. Hugo was leaning back, with his hands behind his head, his face half hidden by the cushions, "I think he may be a spy."

"Well . . . *yes.*"

"By that, I mean to say I don't think he's a proper private detective. I believe he's a spy."

"A spy? *A spy?*" she repeated, with total incredulity, "What the hell is he spying on?"

"I think he's spying on me."

A chill of terrible disquiet was upon her. "Why should he be? But you must have sent him to Hunt's digs and everything?"

He got up again, as if he couldn't bear the conversation dragging on, and stared out of the french windows, with his back to her.

"Why should he spy on you? Or me? Why did you hire him?"

"Nella, I don't know yet. I can only say I went along with his private eye idea because it seemed so preposterous. Clover introduced himself very casually — he was always hanging about the PDSA and we had several talks about records. When I said you were off to Liverpool, he told me he was. He insinuated and suggested and made me suspicious so I fell in with it. He seemed to know too much about us. I wanted to wait and see if he was up to anything."

She felt herself flushing. "Why didn't you tell me?" Was it true? Was he having a breakdown? It was Hugo who thought Mrs Pope was attempting to poison him. Could it be the chicken bones? "But I don't understand why Eric Clover should want to spy on you."

He swung his club and tapped a ball smartly across the floor. "No, it is a bit far-fetched."

"Have you been doing anything secretive?"

Hugo looked amused and pleased with himself and exceptionally secretive. "Only the occasional small courier service for a friend when I'm away sometimes. It's nothing. No danger."

"You promise?"

"Sure."

"Hugo, never do anything."

His golf ball clacked back and forth across the polished floor and she wasn't sure whether or not she'd let out a tiny cry or whether it was only in her head. Stumps. Spies. It wasn't real life anymore. "I beg you with all my heart, please don't get involved with anything . . . *anything*, will you."

"Maybe he is a private eye. We'll see. I'm sorry to do this to you."

"As long as you realise you're finishing us with all this nonsense. It's what you did to Barbara about her mother."

"It needn't affect you. I'm only asking you to behave normally." His tone was completely reasonable. "If you talk to Clover, try and find out a bit more about him.

Has he been trying to worm his way into your acquaintance?"

"Yes."

"I can't put my finger on it yet. He might be a blackmailer. I wouldn't let him into the house, if I were you, but I don't believe you're in danger so don't worry about that."

She stared at him, speechless. Eric Clover was in her mother's house at that moment. She'd left him minding the cat.

She felt as if she was reeling. Did Hugo know she'd been writing the reports herself? Did he know what was happening with Eric Clover? Did he believe all this stuff he was telling her? She couldn't believe it. It must be Robin Stewart White he was worried about. He'd always lived in dreams. When he stopped being a conjuror, he simply carried on fantasising in everyday life.

There was nothing more to be said. She'd taken them to the edge. She could hardly reassure him about Robin when there was Eric. She hadn't the strength left to say the things that would take them over it.

Bad Dog pushed his head against her knee and held up his paw. Her throat was hurting again as she pressed her mouth against his flat silky head. There were lines, she'd read once, about a dog being man's best friend but woman's consolation in the end. Whoever thought of that knew what they were talking about. She stood up to start the washing up.

"What is wrong, anyway?" Hugo asked, a while later, as he helped her to put the dishes away.

"What?"

"What do you want from your marriage to me? Or what did you want?"

Touched that he was pondering on it, she smiled even though it was too late.

"What I would have liked, you know," she answered, sitting down at the table again and resting her cheek on her hand, "was to be cherished. That's wishing for perpetual romance. I wonder if anybody ever does feel they've been cherished.

"My feeling about you is that you're a loner. What makes living with you extremely desolate is that you're like a dog on the edge of the pack. A dog who needs affection and looking after but who won't come near enough to get it. You've accused me of things but you can't receive affection . . . well, you can't from me.

"Another thing," she said, into the silence, "is I suppose I've felt inadequate really to be in this house without children. No, no, it isn't that . . . I know what it is. I know what I would have liked. It would have been to be . . . um, a small pillar of the community, to have a house with people milling in and out for friendship and reassurance and all that. I wish you'd been a person who would have welcomed them." She turned so he wouldn't see her face getting wet, "I . . . well what I expected was for it to be like home . . . s . . . sort of slow and hab . . . habitual with an entourage of regular people who hadn't got anybody but us. People like Uncle Victor belonged to us . . . or Uncle Hunt and Willie Crook. What did you want?"

"I just wanted you," he said. "But you loved Stewart White."

Chapter 7

Eleanor suspected everything about Eric Clover now even though he actually looked like a private eye and certainly had all the right ingredients. He could have played the part to perfection in a television series. Her moods towards him swung between fear, fascination and scorn. One minute she dismissed the idea that he was a spy as Hugo's nonsense. Real spies were scholarly, effete and full of ruthless ideology. The next minute she was waiting to catch him carrying a poisoned umbrella.

"Hugo's told you about Robin Stewart White, I can tell," she said. "That's what he's interested in, isn't it? I'm not entirely unastute, you know. Well, he's not here. Hunt thinks he's coming to the hospital but he's not here any longer. I haven't seen him for years. *Years.*"

One thing was odd. How did Eric have so much time for her? No, it wasn't the amount of time exactly. It was absence of routine. He never talked about this survey thing he was meant to be doing. He hadn't told her anything about it. On the other hand, she hadn't asked, because she knew it was a gigantic Merseyside leisure study and she couldn't be bothered to hear about it. Traitors were misfits, of course. Well, if he was a traitor, she would denounce him. He'd get no further information out of her. She watched him for a while as he read the sports pages in the Sunday paper.

"Were you being a private eye in your marriage?" she asked.

"Yes . . . why? I did some jobs."

"What was your marriage like?"

"Boring."

"But you said you were sorry when she left you."

"I know, I went frantic." He looked up, with a sheepish smile, innocent as a gigolo, "I went to see a shrink in the end because I was such an emotional wreck. I shouldn't tell you what he said about me. It's so uncomplimentary. You'd see me in an even worse light."

"I don't expect so."

"I've never told anyone."

"What did he say?"

"I'm not telling you."

"Eric, don't be silly. Come on."

"It might put you off me for ever."

"I'll be more put off if you don't tell me."

"That shrink said to me, 'We don't usually show patients the reports we make on them but in your case I am going to make an exception.' The report said this guy thought I was a liar, a pervert and a psychopath. That in his opinion I would never change and there was no chance at all of me ever having a satisfactory relationship."

"Crumbs," she said, shaken.

He laughed. "I thought that would shock you. I was stunned myself."

He went back to his paper and she tried, with considerable difficulty, to marshal her thoughts. Where was her mother's blue vase? It had gone! She got up and strolled towards the window, establishing that it was there, not quite in its usual place. So he'd moved it. Had he or had she? Their existence in this glass box was becoming more and more bizarre. On the other hand, wasn't it reassuring? Wouldn't somebody leading a double life wish to keep all this appalling information to himself?

"Why did you approach me then?"

"What?"

"Why did you approach me in the first place? Did you set it up with those men?"

"What are you talking about?"

"Did you know those two men in the grocery shop? Did you arrange for them to accost me?"

"Give it up! I was as shocked as you were by that business. When I saw an opportunity to act, I did. I've told you a hundred times, silly woman. I liked you."

"But if you weren't able to have a normal relationship with anyone, what did you think you were going to involve me in?"

"What's normal?"

"It's irresponsible of you. You pushed me into having a relationship when you're not able to have one."

He sighed. "I've had many relationships. Some more successful than others."

"All disastrous, you mean."

"I wish I'd never been honest with you."

"You bludgeoned me into this. You marked it out for disaster. You picked a married woman, years older . . . uninterested in you . . . well, at the time . . ."

"Ah, but I lived in hope. A good reason could have been I recognised another nutcase."

She brooded, dissatisfied, magnetised like a child to provoke for reassurance. There was something extremely irritating about the way he was lounging about . . . curls dropping over his forehead, the too-glossy clothes, the hairy wrist and big winking clinking watch strap. He was a blob and pleased with it.

"Your hair needs cutting," she said. "Would you like me to do it for you?"

He didn't answer.

"I think I'll do it right away."

She returned with a towel, a comb and scissors. He glanced at them, then at her, with a cool enquiring look.

"Can you sit back a bit in the chair, please?" she went on, placing the towel round his shoulders. "Your left side looks a bit easier. I'll start off there until I get into the swing of it. Now, sit up, will you."

Obediently, he shifted himself into a straighter position and went on reading.

She combed out a wedge of his dark springy hair and cut sideways across it, quite close to the head, so there was no going back. "Mm . . ." she said, standing away from him before boldly shearing the next bit. "You know I think it's going to look very nice."

He glanced at the carpet to see what was happening.

"You shouldn't have it all over your ears. It's far too long. Short back and sides is what is fashionable now. I find it most sexual."

He put an arm out and ran it up the inside of her thigh.

It took her nearly an hour to cut his hair. Happily, the curl in it disguised her lack of expertise. She patted and snipped until she was satisfied.

"I'm afraid you haven't many curls left," she admitted, crouching in front of him to study the effect and meeting his steady meditative stare. "It is short but you do look most beautiful!"

She started piling the hair on the carpet on to a sheet of

newspaper. As she stood up to take it out of the room, he got up too.

He went out to look at himself in the cloakroom mirror.

"Okay, now it's your turn," he said, steering her gently into position, sitting on the chair. He pushed his hands underneath her thick fawn hair and bounced it thoughtfully.

"Oh, I don't want mine cutting."

"I don't remember you asking my permission either," he replied, arranging the towel round her shoulders.

She jumped up, with a squawk of laughter, and pushed him away. "No, no, Eric. I'm not having it!"

He went into the kitchen and reappeared with one of the old dog leashes. He led her to a straight-backed chair, drew her arms round the back of it and tied them at the wrist to the carved spokes.

"Fur's fur," he said in an amused voice, and he began to comb her hair with long slow strokes as if deciding what to do about it.

"Don't cut much, will you. You said you liked women with long hair."

He drew out the first lock to its full length almost touching her shoulders and cut it off at mid-ear. He held it out for her to see.

"I promise I'll do anything in the world if you stop now."

He tilted her head over to the right and her hair began to fall on to her knees in soft mounds.

"Please . . . oh my God. Oh, I . . . help. Let me look!"

"Keep still. No use pleading with me. I'm the Iron Man, remember?"

"But I'll have to go to a hairdresser now."

"Not after this, you won't, Hobbs. As we used to tell 'em in the Army, you'll find this haircut very good value because most of it is coming off."

"You did this in the Army?"

"Right. Part of the initiation ceremony."

She moved to hinder him but he held her head between his fingers and thumb and tipped it deftly forward so that he could work on the back. When she felt a lightness and the air on her neck, she knew all her hair was gone. His fingers pressed into the nape of her neck as he held up the short ends and clipped them close.

She strugggled to free her hands.

"Keep still. You're not done yet."

"Oh please . . . Eric, it's enough."

"Sit up."

He cut the sides shorter to show her ears. At last he lifted the towel from her shoulders and untied her wrists. He led her out to the cloakroom mirror.

He had done to her what she had done to him. Her hair was gone. It flopped on to her ears from a centre parting like a boy's and that was all there was to it. She put her hand up to feel the back where he'd cropped it so severely into her neck.

"Well, you asked for it, as you're fond of saying," he told her apologetically, "and now you've got it."

She stared at him in the mirror. Her lips parted and no sound came.

"You're in my power, aren't you?" he added wonder-, ingly, kissing her bare neck. "I can tell by your eyes."

"I like your new hairstyle," Evelyn volunteered at the hospital. "Very shick."

Uncle Hunt endorsed that. "I like it too, sweet."

"Bill's not eating," she said. "He sleeps all the time. His visitors come then he drops off again. It's no fun for me."

Hunt smiled and nodded ruefully.

"Have you had some visitors?" Eleanor asked quickly, turning enquiringly to Evelyn.

"Bill often has a visitor," she said.

"Is that Robin?"

"I haven't seen anything of Robin lately," he said. "I'd like to go to the lavatory, Nella, if you wouldn't mind."

Tackling the lavatory was something Eleanor dreaded and Hunt's requests to go were becoming more frequent.

She knew how to angle the wheelchair in order to haul him up and hold on to him. That was not easy. While he did it, they rocked together on his one leg, urine soaking his trousers and trickling on to the floor. Thin as he was now, his weight left her gasping.

"When I get back to Mrs Ormer, I'll be able to deal with things a lot more easily," he said.

Eleanor agreed with him knowing he could never go back to the digs. He needed constant nursing care.

That boarding house, with all the old men, was the last stage in his downfall. Eleanor's mother had found him a room with Mrs Ormer years ago when he lost his pub. It had been his home ever since but for one dramatic flight lasting a few weeks.

Seven men lived in the house. They ate together at the dining room table with Mrs Ormer officiating from the adjoining kitchen. All were called by their surnames and Mrs Ormer was called Ormer. Nicknames were used behind backs. For instance, there was Cracky Carter, Cakey York and Uncle Hunt was Dozer Quinton. By that time, he was in a daze of utter melancholy.

"He's lucky to get it," Eleanor's mother kept saying at the time. "Rooms at Mrs Ormer's are hard to come by."

Eleanor remembered baiting Mrs Ormer in her earliest school days when she ran a cafe going down to the shore and sold ice-cream through a hatch. They used to stop on their way home to ask for beige lollies. This request, accompanied by stifled guffawing, never failed to rouse Mrs Ormer to a deliciously terrifying truculence.

Hunt was not grateful for his good fortune in finding a comfortable room at a reasonable price. He made no attempt to disguise his depressed moods and make pleasant conversation at the table. He regularly said 'Balls!' when someone ventured an opening observation or 'Tell that to the Pope!' to stir up Cracky Carter, who was a Roman Catholic.

Mrs Ormer put up with his complaints about her food ('Do we get a prize, Ormer, if we find a piece of meat in this stew?'), because even at his lowest ebb he'd managed to beguile her too. He assisted with the washing up and listened sympathetically, with little far away moos, to all her problems. What she couldn't put up with were his lavish helpings of butter, sugar, and mustard or his impromptu invasions of her cupboards. She started to ration the lodgers by putting helpings straight on to the plates. When Huntly Quinton fell from the top of the stairs to the bottom, Mrs Ormer and Cracky Carter assumed he'd had a stroke.

In the first gloomy days of his life at No 23 Heatherdell Road, when he seemed to be totally cast adrift from his old existence, the one person who livened him up was Robin Stewart White. In those days Hunt talked often of making a new start in London and Robin encouraged him. A job could easily have been found in his father's firm but

Eleanor knew Robin was far too careful to let himself be too seriously embroiled with Huntly Quinton's drinking, amused as he might be by an evening out with him. And there were plenty of those.

"I think old Robin should come up with something for me soon," Hunt kept saying hopefully. "He's a good egg."

Eleanor was thinking of going to London herself by then. Her relationship with Robin had improved. As her confidence grew, their age gulf was diminishing. At last he'd told her he loved her, explaining that he'd had to conquer emotional difficulties of his own, concerning someone else. So she felt they were nearly there. As soon as the right job came up, she would go, and then they could be together.

On two or three evenings a week she had jobs for the paper but, most weekends, with Hugo gone, if Robin was abroad, her life fell back into its childhood routine.

A muted Uncle Hunt came on the bus for supper on a Thursday but at weekends he was there all day, padding about with the wheelbarrow and rake, and pulling up plants. Her father's great friend, Victor Jennings, always came too for Saturday tea and Sunday tea and supper. A recluse, who'd retired at twenty-four, Uncle Victor arrived on an ancient Raleigh bicycle, bringing cuttings from the *Daily Telegraph* for Eleanor's mother. His self-appointed job was to mow the grass. After tea he and Norman Mackie had putting competitions for small stakes, and after supper they played ping-pong. Uncle Willie Crook only came for a drink because he had his architectural practise to think about, Lutyens' houses (be they in Sussex or Simla), to be visited, and seventeen cats to look after.

A usual Sunday supper was Eleanor's father's favourite

fish cakes. What was not usual was an upset at the table. Eleanor might have created one from time to time but nobody else ever did.

On this evening, at the end of the fish cakes, Norman Mackie stood up to recite some of Billy Bennett's music hall verses, humour his wife did not in the least appreciate. Eleanor didn't find them funny either but from the moment he cleared his throat and shouted in the Billy Bennett manner, 'She was only a postman's daughter but, my, how she sorted the males!' all three men laughed till they cried. Forced tears, Eleanor suspected, flowed down her father's cheeks.

Into this lopsided atmosphere, a remark was made about bull fighting.

"The Spanish must be scum," her mother declared sharply. "Bull fighting is barbaric. Only scum would put it on for entertainment."

"It's a wonderful spectacle," Hunt responded, with his loyalty to all things Latin.

Eleanor joined in immediately. "But the horses get gored as well. How can you? Their vocal chords are cut so they can't be heard screaming."

"Nella, I'm not saying it's a good thing," her uncle replied carefully, "I'm only telling you what a colossal spectacle it is."

She and her mother fell on him protesting at his cruelty. Norman Mackie kept quiet because he was the most fervent animal lover of all time. Victor Jennings tried to change the subject.

"Well, anybody who defends bull fighting is finished as far as I'm concerned," Eleanor's mother exclaimed.

"It's a matter of opinion," her brother insisted dourly.

"If that is your opinion," she said, "you'd better go."

"I'm going." He pushed his chair back and stood up. "And I'll tell you something. I've had all the people in this place right up to here. They're dead from the neck up. That's what's wrong with them. They've got their houses and their cars and they think they're really something. But I don't give that for them," he added, making a snapping noise with his fingers.

He was a few minutes collecting his coat and cap from the cloakroom while the two women waited in the hall to see him off. Both brother and sister regretted the exchange which was about more than bull fighting. What exasperated Eleanor's mother was the streak of genial credulousness which enabled him to see no wrong in a bull fight. That same streak had caused him to spend his days buying drinks for deadbeats, and made him a target for financial twisters, and brought him to his present penniless pass. In his turn, he'd been trying to keep his end up. There was a brief parting of mutual dudgeon then Madeleine Mackie said, "Come on Thursday."

"I will. Many thanks. Nighty night."

There was enough of it left for him to get completely plastered at the pub on the way home.

When he let himself in to 23 Heatherdell Road, he could hardly see, let alone stand, and he was immensely depressed. Everybody was in bed and the house was dark and still. He felt his way along the landing wall to find the light switch and banged his knee against the telephone table. He had no idea where his room was. With a blasphemous curse, he blundered into Mrs Ormer's bedroom.

Although Iris Ormer was a huge woman, with legs like columns and an affronted face of paratha texture, it would not have been the first time one of her lodgers attempted to have his way with her.

141

Breathing audibly down his nose, Huntly Quinton was weaving his way unsteadily towards her as she threw back the blankets and semi-sprang from the bed in a voluminous Viyella nightdress.

He bumped right into her, his bulk knocked her back, then he sat on her. "Whoopee," he said, without animation and purely out of habit, being a person who welcomed company. "Applee pee!"

His shoes dropped off one after the other as he sat contemplating the darkness. "Life's a funny thing, you know. One minute you're up. The next you've had it."

Mrs Ormer heaved beneath him. "I don't allow men in my room."

He grunted moodily. "Is there a man in your room, Mrs Ormer? If only I had sixteen fists, I'd clout him with every one of them at the same time."

He stood up, swayed, then he removed his coat, and belched. He loosened his tie and started to undo his shirt buttons.

"Don't you dare take your clothes off."

Breathing heavily above her, he pondered what to do. He was too chivalrous to reveal how appalled he was to find his landlady lying in wait in his bed. On the other hand he could not face love play.

"Why don't I just climb in in my bathing costume?" he suggested helpfully. "As a matter of fact, I'm exhausted. I must get some sleep."

"Get out of my bedroom. I'm giving you a month's notice."

He belched again. "Done. Quite right, Ormer. I was hoping you'd say that so let's shake hands on it. I don't blame you. Tell those Joe Citizens at the breakfast table that I'm going to London and I bid them all a very goodbye.

I can't say I've enjoyed knowing them because I haven't. They're all awful. And Fred French with his blooming zimmer, taking all morning to come downstairs, is the worst." He put his hands out to find the door handle and knocked a knick-knack off her bedside table. Anxious to avoid further unpleasantness, he went over to the window. Forgetting he was not in his own room, which opened on to a small balcony, he clambered over the sill and fell twenty feet into the dahlias.

He went to London then. Eleanor's parents were dead against it.

"Don't lose Mrs Ormer's good little room," her mother pleaded. "You'll never find another."

"He'll be back, of course," said her father.

"I've got to go, Norming," he exclaimed, "I've heard of a billet in London. Assistant manager at the Thrale Hall Hotel, Streatham. It's a start, isn't it. I know the trade. I should be pretty useful to them while I'm looking out for something else."

"He'll be tight from morning to night," Norman Mackie prophesied.

With a generous flourish, and despite their protestations, Hunt distributed most of his remaining belongings among the family because he needed to travel light. A rug went to Eleanor's mother, an umbrella to her father. A small coaching print was left for Eleanor. "And I'd like old Vick Jennings to have my compass," Hunt said. "Useful for his cycle rides. It's always worked very well."

The thought of him in Streatham still amused her.

"D'you remember when you took off for Thrale Hall?" she reminded him. His head was nodding on his chest. Music and television gunfire, plus the hot sweet atmosphere of old age in the Day Room, was making her sleepy as well.

"Ooh yes! Madre Mía!" He drew in his breath with one of his most wicked smiles. "What a shocker that was!"

He moved his left leg, which was swinging down on to the floor, feeling for the wheelchair step. The stump of his right leg, stitched up at the end like a German sausage, bobbed outside the blanket. She got up to guide the foot back on to the step and tuck the blanket into position. He looked so gaunt and grey. "I think you're tired today, aren't you?"

"He's sleeping all the time," Evelyn stated again. "He's not eating."

"To tell the truth, Nella, I am tired. I think I'd like to go to bed now."

"I'll ask the nurses to help me."

"I wanted a word with you, dear," the Sister said. "Bill's not too grand. He's not eating because he's had a chest infection for the past few days. He's still got some fluid on his lungs so we want to keep him sitting up."

Eleanor was half-expecting the call from the hospital when it came about eleven o'clock that evening.

Eric Clover was in bed. Eleanor was lying on top of it, partially undressed and giggling, making up some colourful happenings for herself for Hugo.

"That'll be Hugo," Eric said.

As she lifted the telephone, he seized her discarded pants and covered his face like a sunbather.

"We're concerned about your uncle's condition," the Sister said. "He's not very well."

"You're ringing because it's serious?"

"He's worsened since you saw him earlier, dear."

"Ought I to come right away?"

144

"Come as quickly as you can. The doctor's with him now."

Eric Clover drove like the wind.

As they turned off the main road, and the hedges of narrow country roads closed in upon them in the headlights, she knew she'd remember the strange numbing atmosphere of this night drive to hospital for the rest of her life.

When they got there, she went in on her own.

"He's very poorly indeed," the nurse whispered, "I'm glad you managed to get here. He's not likely to go through the night. I'll bring you a cup of tea."

In the half-light of the sleeping ward, one or two wakeful old men greeted her. Hunt lay on his back. His mouth was open, slewed and sunken. His breathing was fast and loud and there was a peculiar phlegmlike rattle in his throat.

"Uncle Hunt . . .?" she said, taking hold of his thin fingers, "I'm here. It's Nella." She thought his fingers tried to curl round hers but his eyes didn't open.

The nurses brought the tea and drew the curtains round the bed. Eleanor sat quite still in that isolated little cubicle as the night ticked away. She was hunched over, watching him and waiting. Occasionally she moved to stretch her legs and she left him once to go and telephone her mother in New Zealand.

What was she meant to be doing while he was slipping away? She must not draw him back. She had to let him go and she had a strong sensation that he had already gone. She leant forward and spoke so quietly her message was no more than a whisper. "You are the best uncle anybody ever had," she said, to send him on his way. He went on breathing but she knew he hadn't heard her.

She sat beside him for three hours; then the crisis passed and he opened his eyes.

"How are you feeling?" she asked, hoping he wouldn't find anything odd in seeing her there in the middle of the night.

He smiled, his same old smile as if he was including her in a load of naughty tricks. "I feel a bit cheap, sweet."

"Your chest infection will have exhausted you. Well, you're much better now. What can I get? Is there anything you fancy?"

"I'd like a peppermint, please."

She opened the bedside drawer and got out the sweet tin.

"You know, Nella, I've had the most extraordinary experience," he mused, wonderingly. "I was dashing about in space. When I came back into the hospital again, everything was going on exactly as before."

She knew he'd died. She smiled, longing to ask what dying was like. "Well, you've been dozing a lot, haven't you. I expect you've been dreaming."

"Yes I have. Was Robin here?"

"No . . . if I see him I'll tell him you haven't been well."

"Do that small thing," he replied. The words stayed in her mind because his voice sounded slightly mocking.

Chapter 8

Uncle Hunt had always seemed a bit ambivalent about her relationship with Robin. It was as if he had one attitude from the point of view of his own friendship with Robin and a different attitude for hers. Occasionally he'd say something, if there was an opening, as if he guessed it wasn't going to turn out well and he felt responsible.

"Robin's a wonderful cove but I think he's a bit old for you, Nella, that's what worries me. He could spoil your life."

She'd skip off, beaming like a mad thing, at the sound of Robin's name. "I'll be the judge of that!"

Her uncle never intervened until the weekend he was fired from Thrale Hall and she and Robin went to France together.

Eleanor's father had been right. Huntly Quinton was tipsy at the hotel from morning till night. The manageress hovered at his shoulder, finding fault, as he went about his duties. The job lasted three weeks then he returned to Mrs Ormer's, taking back all his possessions, except the compass, which Victor Jennings had unfortunately given away for Lifeboat jumble.

The day he arrived home again, her parents were away. Eleanor received a long distance call in the office where she was in the middle of writing up some cases from the Magistrates Court.

"What ho, Nella!" She knew that jovial shout. It meant he'd had a few.

"Hallo, Uncle Hunt."

"What ho . . . !"

"Where are you?"

"What's that, sweet?"

"Where are you?"

"I'm at Euston, sweet. I'm on my way!"

"How's the job? Is it nice?"

"I'm sorry to say the job's over. I should not have gone to Thrale Hallington. Look, I can't get hold of Ma. D'you know where she is? I was wondering if I could stay the night while I square Mrs Ormer about my old room?"

"Yes, come . . . fine. Ma and Pa have gone to Shap till next week so I'll be on my own. Robin's off on . . ."

"Robin's in bad odour. He's not . . ." The line was crackling. She could hear train noises. "See you later, Nella. Whizzo . . . applee pee!"

"Applee pee."

As she put the telephone down, it rang again.

"City Desk?"

"Yes it is," she replied, in a melting voice. She was smiling happily, eyeing the Chief Reporter, Marcia Molyneux, to see if she was registering another private call. "I thought you were in Germany."

"So I was," Robin replied. "Now I'm back in London and suggesting you come to France with me for the weekend."

"Oh." She gave a wistful little laugh. "I can't. What a pity . . . Ma's away! I haven't got a passport."

"Really not? Blast! Oh, look, we'll have to get you through somehow . . . just come."

"Can't you come here?"

"I'd rather go to France."

She hesitated. "I'd better come, I suppose," she said, "hadn't I?"

"I hope so. It's up to you. We'll take the aeroplane to Le Touquet and have dinner."

The same glossary of Eleanor's mother's phrases naturally applied even more to girls who went away alone with men than to girls who didn't stop men touching their busts. She'd wanted to be a virgin when she got married. Eleanor could hear her mother's tombstone voice most clearly as she wavered and Robin waited. 'Disgraced . . . it always gets back. A laughing stock . . . branded for all time.'

"I'd love to come," she said, unable to resist the thought of sitting beside him as he flew the plane. "Uncle Hunt will be staying in the house so that's all right." She felt sorry to be leaving Hunt alone just when he needed consolation.

It was a thrilling moment. Burning her boats.

That weekend put paid to her relationship with Robin. Her mother would have said it was because she went away with him, cheapening herself and shocking everybody else to the core. It wasn't that, she knew, although even Uncle Hunt had looked extremely taken aback when she told him where she was going.

What was wrong was wrong almost from the moment Robin met her at the station. She caught sight of him, lounging with his mature London assurance, at the barrier. He was tapping the end of a rolled-up newspaper on to his hand as the passengers poured off the train and up the platform towards him. As she took some deep breaths, the sun focused suddenly into a golden radiance on his white hair. How she adored him! Inside her head, Ella

Fitzgerald sang out in triumph, as the orchestra swelled. *They'll never believe . . . that out this great big world you've chosen me.* Filled with joy, she moved faster. He saw her and raised his paper in greeting.

"Nella, hallo." He took her case and held her hand as he kissed her. "How lovely you look, as always. How was the journey?" To her chagrin, she could tell he was quietly amused by her little brown travelling hat with wings over the ears.

"It was fine." Instantly, she felt a bumpkin. "Too crowded though so I had to go into a first class to get a seat. Luckily the ticket collector let me off. Anyway, I was only planning to say I hadn't any money and offer my name and address."

"Jolly good, another helpless Nella Mackie fan bites the dust!" His smile creased into the teasing, well-marked lines of older skin as it did in the best part of all her daydreams. "So . . . now, we'd better get back to the flat, change into something more comfortable, have a quick drink and speed out to the airport."

Robin lived in a rather gloomy West End flat, roomy and masculine, above the chemist, John Bell and Croydon, in Wigmore Street. The entrance, with a stately porter who conducted them to the lift, was round the corner in Welbeck Street. Eleanor had been most curious to see it. More conservative than she'd imagined, it was obviously furnished with old family pieces of mahogany. The atmosphere was as neat and lifeless as the Stewart Whites' functional office flat in Liverpool, as if he was too often away or eating out. The only lived-in signs were the open drawers and bundles of discarded clothing in the bedroom of his nephew, Tony Piercy, who shared the flat and whose room she used to change in.

"Tony is in my blackest books," Robin was frowning as he came out of the kitchen with a note in his hand. "The silly fool has offended Mrs Kelly again. She's my marvellously reliable daily. She's been coming for years and I'm not going to lose her because of Tony's behaviour. He'll get his *congé* before she does, if he's not careful."

"What's happened?"

"She's complaining." He went to a corner cupboard for glasses. "Scotch? It suits me to have him in the flat when I have to be away so much but he's jolly naughty with her. I expect he's had girls here when I've specifically told him away games only."

"Robin!" Eleanor, a stranger to games home or away (excepting an hour or two on the bed with Hugo Hobbs with her pants on), gave a squawk of worldly laughter. She swung back on the sofa, crossing her long legs in a dashing manner and blew out another uninhaled puff from her cigarette holder. "How could you? Poor Tony. How unfair!"

"If he wants to do that sort of thing, he can go to a hotel. He upsets Mrs Kelly. He starts giving her all sorts of orders, asking her to make toast and so forth." He glanced at the note again and put on a strong Irish accent to imitate Mrs Kelly. "I can't stand that Mr Tony with his smart and smirking ways."

Eleanor laughed too but she did it with a faint chill. Was that why they were going to a hotel — to have an away game?

In retrospect, she blamed her own unhingement, naturally. But she kept trying to work out exactly when it had gone all wrong. She analysed it, a thousand times, in the months afterwards.

When they set off to drive to Croydon Airport, Robin

was being his usual calm, concerned self — even more so — but he seemed preoccupied. He felt aloof from her. She thought he was still thinking about Mrs Kelly and Tony Piercy and deciding what to do about it.

She broke the silence. "What are you going to do about it?"

"Do about what?"

"About Mrs Kelly and Tony."

"Oh, that. Nothing. I'm just going to warn Tony to behave himself."

"Is anything else the matter?"

"No." He glanced at her, looking markedly puzzled, "Nothing's wrong. Why should it be?"

She stayed silent for a minute, depressed by the start of their weekend and the stringy dreariness of the suburbs going out of London. The traffic was terrible. An oily smell hung heavily on the air.

"But we've got out of communication."

"You worry too much," Robin replied, radiating aloofness. "It'll be all right."

'Will it? Will it though? Will it be all right?' She nearly couldn't stop herself actually saying it. If she asked it once, she'd ask and ask and the insecurity would mount as his responses grew more brief and impatient.

Maybe he had to get used to the idea of having her in London with him? Or was he already despising her for being involved in an away game?

Her chat wasn't amusing him as it usually did. She started to tell him about Uncle Hunt leaving the hotel and going home.

"I know about that," he said, quickly, and changed the subject. He obviously couldn't stand hearing about the latest Hunt catastrophe. He loathed the drinking.

They were all right again when they arrived at the airport and she saw his little aeroplane. It was a Percival Gull with four seats and toylike in its primitive discomfort. It was like being in a buzzing bubble. Flying beside Robin was such an excitement, she thought of nothing then but the joy of it. They buzzed above toy fields, dived down lawlessly low over toy people and Robin stopped the engine, let them drop and started it again. They had no fear of flying.

She passed into France easily at his side.

"My wife has left her passport behind," he said laughing and shrugging with the French official at the hopeless ways of women.

It was dark by the time they ate. All she remembered of that October night with Robin in Le Touquet was falling in love with all the coloured shutters, the little restaurant, with its special French smell, and the proprietor who greeted him as an old friend and gave her long warm admiring looks, as if he put his blessing on their partnership. Their bookings, it turned out, had been made before Robin even invited her. She smiled at that, forgiving him, drowsily content to be taken with the same presumption when they got to bed.

It was twin beds.

"Oh hell," she said, terribly disappointed.

He didn't appear to hear. He was moving about, opening their shutters and looking at the town from the little balcony then he pulled some red silk pyjamas from his bag. "Shall I go first? I expect you'll want to take longer in the bathroom?"

She sat down on the edge of the bed, in her awkwardness, and pretended she was reading a booklet of French instructions. Was she to take longer to look lovelier?

"Sleepy?" he enquired, as he came out again. He went

across to take the other bed, nearest the door. "Bathroom's all yours." He took out a paperback, arranged his pillows, climbed into bed and began to read.

She did take a long time in the bathroom. She had to admit that, afterwards. She wanted their first night to be an extravaganza. She had to compete with older, experienced women who knew what to do in bed and she had to make quite certain he liked being with her best.

She brushed her pale hair back from her face so that it fell forward on her shoulder, brushing the straps of her short amber nightie. Her legs looked very long and slender and her face glowed with excitement. She stepped into the room, with wide serious eyes, hoping he would like the look of her.

He was asleep.

"Robin?"

"Mm?"

Eleanor went across to his bed to kiss him goodnight, sure that he would grip her and pull her in with him.

"Hallo?" His eyes half opened. He lifted his head sleepily, his mouth open, to find hers. He kissed her. "Mm . . . you smell lovely, pussycat. Sleep well . . . got everything you want?"

Bewildered, she went over to her own bed and got into it. She lay stiffly in the darkness.

"Why did you get two beds?"

Silence.

"Why did you get two beds?"

"What?"

"WHY . . . DID . . . YOU . . . GET . . . TWIN . . . BEDS?"

"Because they were available," he answered, speaking into his pillow in a muffled voice.

"That man said this was the room you wanted. You booked it ages ago."

"I thought you'd like it. Be a good girl, Nella. Try and get to sleep. Would you like a pill?"

"A sleeping pill?" she echoed, deeply aggrieved.

"I thought you might find difficulty in sleeping in a strange place."

"There's no difficulty . . ." she started challengingly then her voice trailed off. "It's just you . . ."

"I don't understand."

"You can't just go off to sleep like that." She knew she was yammering babyishly and that older, experienced girls would know how to be attractive enough.

"Don't you want to be treated with respect?"

That stopped her in her tracks. "Yes, *but* . . ."

"But?"

"Well, I'd like my own room, please. Get me another room. I'd rather be on my own."

"If you move out of this room, you can make your own arrangements and you can pay for them."

She lay completely still, waiting, guessing he'd be shocked by the brutal way she'd spoken.

With a sigh, he swung out of bed and padded across. Gently, he pushed her down into the bed, covered her up and tucked her in. He kissed her again. "Sleep well . . . don't spoil our weekend here. Can I get you anything . . . a glass of water?"

"No."

"Right. Nighty night." With a long-suffering flurry of bedclothes, he flung himself down against the pillow, tossed over and tossed back again. With his head facing away from her, he fell asleep.

She listened to the rhythm of his breathing. He'd said

he'd be available any time she liked. Hot tears trickled down her cheeks and dropped on to the sheet.

Wide awake for hours, she watched him across the room. She was thinking, thinking, thinking what to do. When it was nearly light, she acted suddenly. She got out of bed, stomped straight over and kicked him in the back.

They left Le Touquet practically within the hour. Not speaking.

Robin spoke first at the airport, just as they were getting into the plane to take off for London. "I've got to wipe the windscreen. Can you see a rag there or anything?"

She couldn't. Without a word, she opened her handbag and passed out her emergency sanitary towel.

He thanked her, with a sharp glance from the blue eyes, and cleaned the windscreen. She knew he was amused.

When they were in the air, zooming up and diving down, they looked at each other and smiled. The communication came back again.

She was disappointed to be taken home. Hunt would be there. She would have preferred a day alone in London with Robin but he had work to do, he said, at his Liverpool office on Monday.

"I'd rather not get involved in HQ's drinking, Nella," he said. "Do you mind if we don't?"

"I quite agree," she replied emphatically.

Hunt was of course extremely pleased to see them. It wasn't his business after all to tell Eleanor how to behave, even if her parents were away. They all went out to lunch together at a little place he recommended near Chester.

The outing and the company helped to lift his depression over the Thrale Hall débâcle, although Robin made it clear he wasn't interested in hearing any amusing descriptions of Hunt's period in Streatham. It was an agreeable meal despite the slight stiltedness between the two men because of their temporarily mutual disapproval.

Eleanor felt happy again. In retrospect, rather thankful to be still a virgin. It was after five o'clock when they arrived back.

"That beanfeast was really something," Hunt said appreciatively. "Thank you very much, Robin. A good deal better than Mrs Ormer's fare, I have to admit." He beamed at them. "Vzzzt! Whizzo! Shall we have a small drink?"

"I was just going to make tea, Uncle Hunt," Eleanor answered hurriedly.

"I think I'll stick to the hard stuff, if you'll excuse me." He tiptoed out with elaborate stealth, like a pantomime cat, towards the kitchen, "Pray be good enough to excuse me."

Robin and Eleanor looked at each other. This prim speech was a signal that he was already well underway.

While Robin and Eleanor drank tea, he sat with his glass of whisky beside him, his head bent, ruminating somewhat ponderously on the events of life and his own lot.

"Vzzzt!" he said occasionally, thrusting his jaw out and butting his head, in quite an amicable way. "And you're a good doggie." He tapped one of the dogs with his toe. "What about a spot of music on the old machine, Nella? What's that record you've got . . . 'Truly Truly Fair'. Let's hear it."

With her heart sinking, Eleanor obediently put Guy Mitchell singing 'Truly Fair' on the radiogram.

Uncle Hunt rose to dance to it. Holding the corners of his jacket turned out, he pointed his toe. With his knees bent, in the manner of a man stiff from a horse, he jigged away down the long sitting room, stepping forwards, sweeping backwards, bowing and twirling daintily to the music. " . . .*how I love my truly fair!*" he refreshed himself with a quick swig. "Vzzzt!"

"He'll be turning nasty soon," Robin murmured, as the old record started up again, "I'm not waiting till he starts flinging shoes on the fire. Let's go and have supper in the firm's flat." He stood up.

"What's cooking?" demanded Hunt.

"I'm taking Eleanor to the flat," Robin said, "I want to have a look at some mail before tomorrow morning."

"Good idea," Huntly Quinton glared at them, his forefinger crooked over in the air. "Why don't you?"

While Eleanor got her mother's car out of the garage, her uncle went down to the gate to wave them off. One car came along the road as he stood waiting.

As it passed him, he waved his arms rudely, made a kicking motion and shouted. "Go on. Gid out of it, you broken-down cow!"

The driver slowed down, backed up and wound the window down. "Is anything the matter?"

With a hint of pantomime cattery, Huntly Quinton tiptoed over, holding the corners of his jacket out. "Not at all," he said, in a most polite, reasonable voice, "I'm so sorry. I mistook you for a friend of mine."

"That's all right then," the man replied. "Good night."

"Good night," Hunt replied meekly, but as the car pulled away, he lunged after it, making a V sign. "You've had your chips, chum!" he roared, "so F off!"

"Without drink, Hunt is the most amusing man in the world," Robin remarked, as they drove away.

"I think, the trouble is, he has to drink now before he's amused by anything," Eleanor answered. "What I hate about it is that when he drinks you simply can't get in touch with him."

At the Stewart Whites' first floor flat in Rodney Street, Eleanor made spaghetti for them while Robin looked at his mail and went through some office papers for the morning. They had just started to do the washing up when the door bell rang.

He looked out of the window. "Oh no," he said, clapping his palm against his forehead, "it's Hunt. We're not getting into that. Turn the light out. We'll have to go into the bedroom."

Eleanor took her shoes off and lay on the big bed. She picked up a book from the bedside table and pretended to read but she couldn't focus on the words. Robin stood in the doorway, listening.

The bell rang again.

They waited.

"Hullo!" Hunt shouted from down below in the quiet street of specialists' consulting rooms, "*Robin*! It's Hunt. Can you open the door?"

"Oh my God," Eleanor whispered.

"Forget it," he said. He lay down on the bed beside her and kissed her. "It'll stop in a minute. He'll have to go away."

It didn't stop. He'd give three prolonged rings then there was silence. When they thought he'd given up, the bell went again.

"Robin! Eleanor! I want to speak to you. I know you're in there. Let me in."

"The whole street will be listening to this," Eleanor said. Her body was jumping with nervousness.

Hunt hammered on the door as Robin kissed her again and undid the buttons on her blouse. Leaning on one arm, with his head on one side, he looked bony and intent, as his hand slipped inside and closed over her breast.

"No, no," she said, "not now."

He manoeuvered her arms out of the sleeves of her blouse and undid her bra. She lay still, her eyes wide open with horror, as he stood up and removed his trousers.

The door bell went again. On and on.

"OPEN THAT DOOR! I want my niece out of there in two minutes. I'm giving you TWO MINUTES!"

"Robin, we'd better open it."

"Don't be silly."

"But he knows we're here."

"Take no notice. He'll go." The expression on his face was unforgettable. He stared at her, weighed something in his mind and, with a kind of grim exhilaration, he reached out for her pants and started to pull them down.

"No, no, *no* . . . don't, don't, don't do it, please." She held tight to the pants as he tried to unlock her fingers. He tugged sharply, there was a tearing sound, and he tugged again. "I don't want it like this," she said, struggling, deeply distressed. But he wasn't thinking of her. He was unreachable. His temper lost. She fought against his chest to heave him off.

"You'll be grateful in retrospect, I promise." His tongue flicked out to lick his lips like the wolf in *Red Riding Hood*. The blue eyes had nothing in them. His teeth were showing in a cold contemptuous smile of sex. The yellow between them revolted her.

Twisting violently, she swung off the bed, clutching her clothes. "I'm letting him in."

When she opened the door, neither uncle nor niece said a word. He was glowering blackly, beetle-browed, moving like a bull. She couldn't bear to speak to him. Dishevelled, her face bruised rosy, she led the way upstairs. Though she went into the sitting room, he ignored her. He walked straight into the kitchen where Robin was standing, his back turned, running the water to wash the supper dishes.

"I told you to send my niece downstairs," Huntly Quinton said, straight-backed and stentorian. With a deft movement, he put out a flat hand and swept the coffee cups off the surface beside the sink. They smashed on the floor.

"I've warned Eleanor. God knows why she doesn't have any sense in her head, and now I'm warning you. I told you in the first place to watch your behaviour with her. You're ruining that girl's life." Plates, knives and forks went to the floor in one monumental torrent of noise.

Eleanor stood, transfixed.

Robin said quietly, "Get out of here, Hunt."

"Don't you ever attempt to see her again. D'you hear me? Don't you show your face in this area."

There was a discordant crackling of breaking glass.

Outside in the hall, Eleanor opened her mouth. Some small sound came. Only a sound. She listened again. If she wasn't there, she thought, shivering, it might cease.

On her way down the stairs, she stopped. She heard Robin's voice. "Go. Go now please. You've ruined your own life. You're not going to ruin mine. You don't know the meaning of friendship. You destroy everything you touch."

With her teeth chattering, Eleanor got into her mother's car and drove away.

She tried to see Robin again. She did everything she could think of to put it right. She'd leave it a few months and then make another effort. They became feebler, these ruses, and more humiliating and all the time she knew in her heart it was over for ever.

Chapter 9

"Hugo believes nobody can afford to stay in London hotels now," Eleanor was explaining as she passed things round at Sunday tea shortly before her father died. "Visitors to Britain are booking into Bed and Breakfast places. According to Hugo," she added, smiling at the madness of the statement, "people think nothing of taking rooms as far out as Eltham."

Ninety-year-old Miss Grace Thorogood, founder of her mother's poetry circle, craned forward in her seat, "*Really?*" she queried politely, with an appearance of intense interest.

Uncle Hunt tipped three spoonfuls of sugar into his tea cup, under Eleanor's mother's critical gaze, and stirred it gloomily, old memories of Thrale Hall making him feel even more aggrieved. "Hugo's right, Nella. That's the racket to be in these days. B and B. Get yourselves a suitable house like old Ma Ormer. She must be making a packet out of it."

"Poor Mrs Ormer won't be making a packet," Madeleine Mackie informed him crisply. "She'll be hard pressed to make ends meet, with that house. Cooking and cleaning up after seven men, she'll be on her feet from morning till night."

"True," Uncle Hunt nodded, crushed. He relapsed into silence.

He was in disgrace, in any case. He'd painted the seat of the outside lavatory when he'd been told not to.

Eleanor's father snored, tipped back in his reclining armchair, his mouth wide open and his stick beside him. She knew he'd wake with a start, halfway through tea, and tell them he'd swallowed a ping-pong ball. Willie Crook was beside him, bent over, his legs wide apart, leafing through an antiques magazine and fondling the dogs' ears with his other hand as they milled assertively against him.

"Poor Grace has nothing on her plate," her mother said. "Pass her a scone, will you, Hunt."

Her brother's jaw jutted out a mite closer to bullfrogdom.

"Will you have another scone, Grace?" He stood up and proffered the plate in a rather high, ham-handed manner, rocking slightly.

"Thank you so much." The delicate little hand, muddily freckled with age, slid out for a fourth time. Crumbs scattered from her mouth on to her paper napkin, on to her knees and into her open handbag amongst the balls of used tissue and old pages of poetry notes from past meetings.

"More tea, Vidgie?" Eleanor's mother didn't look at Victor Jennings as she spoke. He'd just presented her with a cutting from the *Telegraph* reporting that Lady Charlesworth had broken her back in the field. Neither of them knew Lady Charlesworth and Madeleine Mackie didn't approve of hunting. When she gave someone a nickname, her daughter had noticed, that person had better beware. It meant she'd had enough of them.

Perhaps she'd grown weary of Uncle Victor's shy eccentric arrivals each weekend, year after year after year even though he kindly provided a Christmas subscription to *Punch* in return. But he no longer came so much since the day, some years earlier, that Eleanor had betrayed him by borrowing his bicycle for a few minutes from outside the kitchen door. It was ironical, she'd thought afterwards, that she should have waited to commit this forbidden act until she was grown up.

"Hugo doing anything interesting at the moment?" Uncle Victor insisted on sitting bolt upright on a hard chair, pulled outside the circle round the fire. Whenever Eleanor looked at him, he made nervous schoolboy gestures over Miss Thorogood's head as she accepted more cake. "We never hear what Hugo's doing. It's a mystery!" He looked about himself with a smile.

"Quite a few international buyers use Hugo now. But he's still inventing his magic stuff," she replied, annoyed. "That's his absolute love, as you know. He's frightfully busy."

Uncle Victor made dolls' house furniture with real lights when she was small. He'd written narrative poems to her at school and sent ten shillings every term. She'd only used his bike to get more hay for Flora from the farm but a sixth sense warned him of the outrage as he watched television and he was waiting at the gate as she pedalled back on the ancient precious Raleigh. The spell was broken. Victor Jennings was a recluse by then having retired originally at twenty-four. It didn't matter that he could have paid for hundreds of thousands of bicycles. It was as if he blamed her parents too for bringing her up so badly she did not grasp the enormity of her action.

His gentle world shattered by deceit, he took to calling as well on Sister Hurst, a nurse at the hospital run by nuns where he'd had a hernia operation. He bought her a budgerigar. He had a little cry when anybody asked after him or Sister Hurst.

Sunday tea people, like Christmas people, had nothing in common. Not interested in each other, they revolved round her mother. Blind Edith, old Rose, Miss Atkins, a nanny from the Quinton childhood who chose to sign her cards 'Botty'. These spinsters had lived on well into their nineties, probably, Eleanor concluded, because they had never known the aggravation from men. When one went, another took her place at tea. Miss Thorogood had been deputy head of St Margaret's, Ruthin. Although the school closed in 1965, reunions continued with Old Girls, now in their sixties, who called her Goody, and were to carry her coffin on their shoulders when she died.

"I ran into Hugo at the Lutyens' exhibition. We had a most enjoyable tea together," Uncle Willie Crook addressed himself in his amiable way to Eleanor and her mother. "Everybody seemed to know him. He's doing very well, I gather."

"I've told Hugo," Mrs Mackie said, "if you raise your hat and open the door for people, you never know what it will lead to."

"Not many people seemed to be wearing hats," Uncle Willie pointed out mildly.

"They're scum," Eleanor's mother said, pouring more water into the teapot. She glared at Huntly Quinton. "They all let the door go in your face these days."

Hunt nodded gloomily. "They do," he agreed.

The talk turned to the new schemes for youth. The perky boys who arrived, on each other's heels, to sell their unwelcome wares and who pressed the bell three times and banged the letter box up and down.

"I've given them eight pounds already this month and

that's their lot," said Eleanor's mother. "They're not getting any more out of me. I can't afford to pay double for a duster, and be diddled over the change. I'm going to tell them."

Grace Thorogood took a sip from her cup which was rocking in the saucer in a pool of tea. "Oh, Madeleine!"

"I'm the only person round here who answers the door now. Nobody else does. They see who it is through the window and they just pretend they're not in. Everybody's terrified."

At that point Uncle Victor went out into the garden again and Uncle Hunt sat brooding while the conversation limped on . . . recent violence on the late trains from Liverpool . . . homos gathering at one in the morning in the men's lavatories near the shore.

"We've got some awful people running this country," Mrs Mackie stated provocatively. "Scum. Things have never been worse."

Miss Thorogood nodded reasonably. "I wonder if that can be true, Madeleine?"

"Two of the softest men I've ever seen, with beards and woolly jumpers, came to the door with leaflets about dog dirt on the pavement. They were standing for the council. I said to them, 'You'll have to find something more important to talk about if you're going to get my vote.'"

"It's a sort of hysteria, isn't it," Eleanor said, "like the smoking frenzy. It's as if the attention of the lynch mob is always being cunningly diverted down a side street."

"All I know is it's hell to take a dog out now. They've put notices all over the park saying DOG FREE AREA and there are bins with black rubbish bags in them. Nobody knows where they're meant to be walking.

There's nothing in the bins either. The black bags are stolen as soon as they're put out."

"Everybody has such big dogs now," Miss Thorogood marvelled.

"Good doggie," Huntly Quinton sat, smoking dreamily. His head was hanging. He was bored stiff.

Eleanor had seen notices down country lanes advertising Rottweiler puppies, bull terriers and Dobermans. They were being bred to fight each other in secret places like the monster lorries parked in lay-bys. A notice in the local pet shop window warned owners their animals might be stolen for use as training bait. Poverty and yobbery, she thought, were a terrifying combination.

"I do think the park is looking particularly lovely at this time of year." Miss Thorogood smiled politely at Uncle Hunt, "Most of the daffodils are out beside the water."

He nodded mechanically. "True." He didn't give a bugger about the park daffodils.

"It brings those well-loved words so much to mind." Her head inclined, she smiled up, coyly, rattling them off, as of yore at St Margaret's. "'Beside the lake . . . beneath the trees . . . fluttering and dancing in the breeze.' Of course you recognise our old friend, don't you!"

Huntly Quinton gazed at her. "Mm . . . what's that, Grace?"

"Our old friend, William Words . . ."

"Oaaah!" It was a semi-shout. As Eleanor's father woke up, he threw himself forwards, his mouth still open, making a sick chortling at the back of his throat.

"All right, dear?" Mrs Mackie enquired soothingly.

"I dreamt I swallowed a ping-pong ball."

Hunt looked sympathethic. "Very easily done, Norming."

His sister gave him a sharp-eyed glance, then another.

"I think you must have had something to drink before you set out?" she asserted, when Grace had gone, with the flat voice of an incredulous victim who has received a blow beyond comprehension. An earlier blow at lunchtime had been the discovery that the gin tasted peculiar. The bottle was obviously watered. "Did you take a drink on your way here?"

"No I didn't."

"You were drinking last night."

"I don't think I . . ."

"People can always tell."

"I may have had one at the Lion," he replied resentfully, "I can't remember."

"I think you must have done," declared the incredulous victim. "I don't know what poor Grace thought. You didn't say a word to her."

"I couldn't think of anything to say. You were talking to her."

"But there's no need to sit there, mute, looking as soft as an owl. You can always think of something. You could have made some effort when she was telling you about the house prices in Medlow Close."

"I don't want to know anything about bloody Medlow Close. I hate it." He laughed, without amusement. "That old woman eats and eats."

"Yes. And you and she both took two bites at your scone in the air. I was a bit fascinated by that. The scone must go back on your plate after one bite unless you want to have no manners."

Manners were the last thing he cared about by that time. He felt so melancholy. He had no conversation, no friends, no money and he'd lost hope. Hope of what? Hope of a new friendship perhaps with another racy little woman, dressed to the nines, as he might have put it. Eleanor supposed. Hope of making another fortune. There's always hope of winning the pools. He hoped that.

Gradually, a sort of majestic bullfrogian gloom descended for ever and he cast it over them all.

"He didn't say a word," Eleanor's father said later. "Did you notice that? *Not a single word.* He can get through two cans of Worthington all right at supper, and he nipped about shutting the windows when he thought my back was turned, but he doesn't make any attempt at conversation. Why does he call me Norming?"

Willie Crook had remained the most active. He'd married late in life, and many children replaced the many cats. His money had dwindled on trips to India to see the architecture but he went on knocking on the doors of Lutyens' houses all over the world. Unable to walk now himself, her father regaled Eleanor with the latest Uncle Willie stories when she came home.

"So he was chatting to this maharaja, who had graciously welcomed his spontaneous visit," Norman Mackie said, tapping his stick on the fireplace with amusement. "Willie happened to glance out of the palace window in time to see his taxi starting up and disappearing with all his luggage. He shouted 'Oh! Look!' Of course the maharaja clapped his hands, gave a speedy instruction and Willie's driver was brought back again!"

But out in his car at eighty-two, Uncle Willie stoved in the side of an ancient Morris driven by two old ladies who were much alarmed by the accident. Willie Crook was taken to court for dangerous driving and told to stop or take a test.

After that his roaming was confined to bus rides to

Liverpool to visit the Picton Library or the Walker Art Gallery. He was in the habit of walking to the bus station and climbing aboard at source. One morning, his wife, Audrey, bound for Liverpool herself, for a day's shopping, got on the same bus as it passed their house. She greeted her husband and sat down beside him.

They bowled along for some minutes in companionable silence and then Uncle Willie spoke. "My wife's got a hat like that," he said.

Audrey was shocked to the core. How could she, with all the other passengers listening, point out that she was his wife?

"Shall we go upstairs?" she suggested nervously.

"You go," he replied pleasantly, "I think I'll stay here. Funnily enough, my wife always likes to go upstairs."

They travelled to town on separate decks and alighted separately. Audrey Crook didn't mention their encounter in the evening.

It was all right when she was in London with Hugo, Eleanor went on living with them all there in her mind. 'Not again!' she'd hear the Captain exclaiming, clapping Uncle Willie on the shoulder, as he removed the golf club copy of *The Field* before the other members had had a chance to read it. After her father died, he still brought it round although her mother had never opened it in her life.

It was Willie Crook's face that Eleanor remembered at her father's funeral. 'Please let me greet all these people properly,' she was praying at the end of the service as she turned out of the pew to walk down the aisle. 'Don't let me cry.' Trying to be brave, she lifted her head. The sorrow in Uncle Willie's eyes across the church was like a shout of pain. He looked like an old dog she'd seen waiting in Battersea Dogs' Home whose heart was broken.

Uncle Hunt was also most genuinely affected but in his case he'd already been knocked sideways and the news sank in slowly. "Well, I'm blowed, sweet. Poor Norming. What a shock," he repeated, two or three times, when she rang Mrs Ormer's house to tell him what had happened.

"That's really damnable about Pa," he summed up, wonderingly, before adding, with a mild note of apology, "On another subject, Nella, I don't seem to have any pyjamas. Do you think you could ask Ma if she's put two pairs in the wash for me?"

Eleanor couldn't help noticing that Eric Clover was no longer being so attentive. He'd begun to disappear for a day or two at a time and Hugo said he wasn't sure but he thought he'd caught sight of him in London.

"Well, nothing's happened, has it?" she said reassuringly. "Nothing's been stolen, he hasn't tried to blackmail or anything. If he's a spy, what's he spying on? He gets nothing out of me."

"So far, so good, yes. Any idea when you'll be coming back?"

"I'm going to ring Ma tonight and see how she's getting on," she replied evasively. "Hunt's in a bad state. Mrs Ormer went yesterday. He opened his encrusted mouth in a huge wet O, held out his arms and said 'Come and kiss me, Stewpot'. He introduced Evelyn as his first wife. Mrs Ormer, I could see, was absolutely staggered at the deterioration. Anyway, he sends his love."

"I want to see Hunt," he said.

"Let's arrange something when I've heard Ma's plans."

"I may have to be away again."

"Well, when?"

"I'll let you know. It's only a little job with some equipment."

"I shan't tell Eric Clover you're going away," she said, teasing him. "You know, you mustn't go on being suspicious. I'm pretty sure he's not interested in us. I mean you. Or me."

Whether he was interested in her or not consumed her now. It crossed her mind that he was a diversion, sent from Heaven, to help her cope. But if he was a diversion, he was a painful one. She waited for him hoping he'd come, excusing the lessening visits and checking the phone was securely on the rest. But it was a game, that was the point. She knew it was a game because she'd taught him exactly how to play it. When he was better at it than she was, it stopped being a game. She was caught in her own trap.

He tested her each time, becoming more brazen.

"Why are you going now?" She began to hear herself, appalled.

"I've got to."

"But I thought you were staying. Look, it's no good if . . ."

He stared at her. His skin seemed to stretch across the wide cheekbones, the nostrils moved in distaste, in place of a curling lip. "Old matrons generally pay me for coming to see them."

She made a sound. When he spoke again, she could hardly hear him.

"Nella, I'll have to borrow your car tonight while mine's at the garage. I've got interviews with a group in Knotty Ash and I'm going to be very late."

"It's my mother's car," she replied, doubting him. "I can't lend it. I'll give you a lift."

The thyroidal eyes clouded. "I've told you, I'm going to be late." He turned away, indifference in his voice. "I'll have to take one of those." He pointed through the windows at a couple of parked cars lit by street lamps. "I know how to steal a car."

She laughed, her legs shaking. "Go on then. Why don't you?"

He picked up the holdall, with some clothes in it, and went out, leaving the front door wide open. A few minutes later, when she heard a car revving up, she followed. Eric Clover had tampered with the lock and broken into a huge white car. Hunched awkwardly inside it, he was whirling the steering wheel. The car suddenly bounded forward and up on to the pavement narrowly missing a street lamp.

"Quick, quick! Come out of it!" She knocked on the passenger window. "Hurry, Eric, get out! You're going to be seen." She gesticulated towards the windows of the houses. Any minute she expected to hear a front door fly open followed by a roar of outrage.

Smirking triumphantly at her reaction, he manoeuvred the car back on to the road. He straightened it up and parked it some distance from its original position.

"But where's your bag?" Eleanor demanded as he came back to the house.

"Hobbs, you're right!" His hand flew to his forehead. "It's in that car!"

As he returned for a second break-in, she left him to it, scurrying into the house, with legs like wool, terrified that someone was watching the whole disgraceful episode from their window.

"I bet your friend Mr Stewart White doesn't know how to start up a locked car, does he?" Eric chucked her under the chin as he held out his hand for the car keys.

'Who dares wins,' she thought resignedly, handing them over. Her nerve had gone. She could no longer bluff to the last. She was too old for it.

"Come back when you've finished your work. It doesn't matter what time," she said, knowing he wouldn't be coming and wishing she could have held her tongue. 'You're acting, aren't you,' she longed to cry out. 'This is a game. I know you're only doing what I taught you . . . so *stop*.'

He didn't come back that night nor was he at his house the next morning.

Convincing herself she had several things to do in Liverpool, that she might even take a job herself, she set out that afternoon to find his office. The truth was she'd had a night without sleep and she wanted to know where he was. The fact that he was out in her mother's car made her ten times more of a fool.

When she got out of the train she walked through to Dale Street because she knew the offices were meant to be just off it. That was all she knew. When she saw the name of the market research company she hoped she'd remember it.

Her father's office had been in Dale Street. It was busy then. She could still hear the bustling steps and feel the air from the Mersey with its oily smell. Why was it evening, with lights, and dank drizzle dulling the shouts of 'Echo Express!'? Queues of cars, headed home, shunted slowly towards the Tunnel. Little smiley Madge, stuffed with old newspaper against the cold, stood squinting on the corner selling Echoes. Eleanor's mother had given her an old fur coat one winter and she'd tied herself into it with string, like a bursting parcel.

Eleanor half-expected to run into her father as she often used to do when she was working. 'How doth the busy bee?' he'd say, raising his hat and smiling at her in his pleased shy way.

The bee was naturally not in the least busy. Merely mooching along to some pointless rendezvous in the North John Street Kardomah.

Gone now.

COMMUNITY RESEARCH GROUP. That was it! She felt certain of it. It looked a big leisurely office as if leisure studies would be going on there. Two girls were fiddling about with parcels in the reception area.

"I'd like to see Eric Clover, please."

"Sorry? Who did you want?"

"Eric CLOVER."

The women glanced at each other.

"Is he here?" Eleanor asked sharply. "This is his office, isn't it?" Another old woman after him, she was sure they were thinking.

"Eric Clover." The older woman looked across at her colleague. "I remember the name. I believe he did do some work for us, didn't he, Karen," she agreed vaguely. "Not recently though." She consulted a list of names on an index by the switchboard. "No, he's not with us now. What sort of work does he do, love?"

"He's interviewing groups of people for a Merseyside leisure study and making an analysis of his findings." Her right leg shook slightly and she shifted her balance to steady herself.

"There's no Merseyside leisure study."

Her mouth seemed to have slewed and stuck in an unnatural smile as if she'd had a stroke. "I was wondering if there would be any work for me?" Fleetingly money seemed her likely saviour from desolation. Even as she spoke she knew there wouldn't be any.

"Have you worked for us before?"

"I haven't any experience."

The receptionist closed her eyes and laughed at the audacity of Eleanor's suggestion. "Ooh no. Sorry. Nothing for you, love."

Nothing for you, love.

Nothing for you, love.

Nothing for you, love.

He was a fake. Hugo'd said he was.

She was sick in the station lavatory. She kept standing up, getting giddy again then kneeling, heaving, her face in the evil-smelling lavatory bowl.

Down on the platform she took long sniffs at the cold train tunnel air. Anguish, guilt and humiliation might not amount to love but they were agony.

At the other end of her journey, she went straight to Eric's house. This time her mother's car was parked outside but nobody answered the door. The old men were deaf. If they had television going in their rooms, they never heard the door bell and Mrs Ormer was obviously out. Eleanor found the kitchen door unlocked at the back and made her way upstairs to Hunt's old room.

She called out on the stairs, and knocked on the door, but there was no sign of Eric. His room was empty.

Hunt's had been the smallest room in the whole house with a single bed fitted neatly beneath the sloping ceiling. There was a slightly fusty smell, what her mother called a fox's lair, as if the window hadn't been opened often enough. It was sad that her uncle's last home should have no atmosphere or feel of him, no smell of Pears soap, laundered shirts or leather, as if that outsize personality had dwindled and dwindled and finally been stamped out.

She sat down on the bed and brought her old exercise book out of her bag. She started a note to Eric then she stopped and put it away. No words were needed for what was going to happen away.

She had spare car keys in her pocket but she took a quick look round in case she could see the ones she'd given Eric. He only had a few possessions in the room. There were three of his modish jackets in the wardrobe and she checked in the pockets of those and in the trousers. She opened a drawer and felt half-heartedly amongst underpants and socks. When she touched paper tucked beneath, she was curious and pulled it out.

An air ticket? Turkey?

Bemused, she regarded the ticket and took deep breaths. Why was he going to Ankara in a week's time? Ankara? He hadn't even mentioned Turkey. Nodding, mentally talking to herself, she smiled, because some point of no return was reached. She stuffed the ticket in her pocket and came out of the room.

From where he was, standing just inside the bathroom door, Eric Clover watched her go downstairs. He listened to her start the car outside and drive away.

Eleanor fed Mungo when she got in. Next, she put the ticket into an envelope and addressed it to Hugo. When that was done, she set out for the hospital. She was in the house no more than ten minutes and, within twenty, she'd stopped at a letter box and sent the communication on its way.

Only Evelyn was in the Day Room, with Ada. "Bill's sick, dear," she annouced sympathetically. "He's been very bad today."

Uncle Hunt was in bed in Dawson Ward. He was asleep lying on his back. Mr Eastwood's bed was empty. The bedclothes folded on top of it. Eleanor quietly moved a chair up beside her uncle's bed and sat down beside him. From time to time a passing nurse would greet her but nearly an hour passed while she simply gazed into space. Hunt woke up just as she had decided to go home again.

He smiled at her. The smile always spread slowly until the whole face was lit up. "Nella!"

"I hear you've had a bad day."

"Pretty bad. I don't know why. I've got a lot of pain at the moment."

He looked so white and gaunt. His nose stood out, with his eyes sunken and luminous. His hands, thin as birds' legs, were plucking at the edges of the sheet.

"Hugo sends his love," she said. "He's coming to see you in a day or two."

"Good-o."

She started to tell him news from her mother but his eyes closed again. "Mm . . .? What's that, sweet?" He dozed for a few seconds. "Applee pee!"

Eleanor kissed his forehead. "Applee pee."

The next day he was up. He was sitting in an armchair in his dressing gown. She sat beside him and he held her hand.

"I'm very very glad to see you, sweet. Thank you for coming." He lifted her hand, in both of his, and bowed his head to kiss it. Again and again, he raised it silently to touch his lips. She knew it was his signal to her that he was at last ready to go gentle into that good night.

He died the next day. The hospital telephoned but she didn't get there fast enough. As she ran down the path to the geriatric wards she knew she was going to be too late. They'd already said goodbye.

The curtains were drawn round his bed and the lights in the ward had been dimmed. It was late in the evening and the old men were settled for the night except for Frank, the blind man with no legs, who was perched on the end of his bed, listening hard.

Eleanor pulled the curtain aside and stopped short, bewildered. There was somebody else beside her uncle. She saw the white hair and thought it was a doctor.

Hunt lay on his back, his eyes closed. The man sitting beside him raised his head and rubbed the tips of his slender fingers across his eye.

"*Robin!*" So he had been coming all the time.

On Robin Stewart White's anguished face she saw the truth she'd never grasped. He'd loved her uncle. Not her.

"He is dead?" she whispered. "You're sure he is?"

"I was here. He was sleeping. He stopped breathing."

The diminished body looked as if he'd left it miles behind. "I'll be outside," she murmured to Robin. "I don't want to stay here."

She and Robin sat in his car and talked until it was light. At sixty, he looked, she decided sadly, a bit like King Penguin. A rather flat-footed walk had developed, with his toes turned out and his head thrown back as if to halt the arrival of more chins. His suit was long and fulsome as if to disguise his shape. He had a marked prissiness, she noticed now. His hair was still flopping abundantly and such a pure glorious white, she guessed it came out of a bottle.

In the veiled unreality of the middle of the night, knocked off balance by losing Hunt, they talked with an ease she'd always dreamed would happen but, in a thousand years, she couldn't have envisaged what they'd be saying.

She said, "You always loved Hunt, didn't you?"

"Always," he admitted, sounding faintly apologetic. "I think I fell in love with him when we first met in a night club in Lima. He pretended he'd been Paul Whiteman's drummer and went up on stage to play the drums. He never loved me in the same way, of course. I knew that. Hunt was totally heterosexual. He blamed me very much indeed for involving you. But I believed it was going to work out for us when I'd managed to conquer my own emotional difficulties. I should have liked a family." He turned to her with sincerity, the eyes blue as ever. "That's what I hoped for."

She nodded, seeing how she could have been quite suitable as next best. "I never believed you were coming to the hospital, you know. Hunt told me over and over again and I assumed his mind was wandering."

"I knew you were coming and I kept out of the way. Sometimes I longed to see you again and talk to you. Other times I was terribly afraid of any dramas at Hunt's bedside. Oh God," he exclaimed wretchedly, pressing his hands against his face. "Life without him is unimaginable, isn't it?"

"Will you be all right?" she asked, knowing he probably wouldn't be all right and there was nothing she could do about it. The sun was starting to come up and the first birds chattered into the silence of the hospital grounds.

"Yes, I'll be all right. I have a pleasant enough life in my village in Wiltshire. My housekeeper does everything for me. You must come and see me soon."

"Yes I must." Perhaps she would. Some day.

"What's the difference," she asked, getting out of his car and shivering in the sharp morning air, "between making love to a man and making love to a woman?"

"Kissing a woman," he said, bending forward to kiss her cheek, "is like kissing a pussy cat."

Chapter 10

Eleanor managed to persuade her mother not to come home from New Zealand for Hunt's funeral.

"What hymns do you think Uncle Hunt would have liked?" she asked, over the telephone.

"'Praise my soul'," Madeleine Mackie answered promptly, picking her own favourites, "And Pam suggests 'Firmly I believe and truly'."

"But he had no belief."

"Well, he will now."

Making arrangements for the funeral was a lot easier than having nothing to do, Eleanor realised. Even the vilely officious woman in the office where she registered Hunt's death must serve a purpose. Quite likely the bereaved broke down, and took hours, if anybody spoke kindly to them.

She hadn't heard from Eric Clover. No doubt he was deeply offended that she'd driven her own car away from outside his house. He might not have heard about Hunt but she was surprised he hadn't been in touch about his ticket to Turkey.

When the doorbell rang halfway through the evening, she ignored it. The curtains were already drawn and she turned the television louder. The bell rang and rang. At last there was silence.

She was waiting for the telephone. At first she took no notice of that either but its persistent ring was nerve-racking. For the sake of peace she picked it up.

"Is that you, dear?" Grace Thorogood said, in her rapid nervous manner. "Eleanor?"

"Yes? Oh, Miss Thorogood! How are you?"

"Thank goodness you're there, dear. There's somebody attempting to climb up the front of your house. I can see him from my window. I've called the police."

Eleanor gasped. "God Almighty! Thank you . . . thanks very much, Miss Thorogood. I hope I know the intruder. I'll fly and see."

She went upstairs, took her shoes off and quietly unlatched the balcony window. It was Eric Clover. He was swinging beneath the balcony, holding on to something and scrabbling for another toe hold. She wanted to reach for the watering can sitting beside the plant tubs and deluge him into orbit. She signalled to Grace Thorogood, peering from her window, and almost laughed.

"Miss Thorogood is watching you," she told him curtly, leaning over and stepping on to his fingers. "She's already called the police. You'd better beat it."

"I'm coming in."

"The police will be here in a minute."

"Where is my air ticket?"

"In the post," she replied, "so that's that and serves you right." Absolutely longing for him, she stepped inside the house and locked the window.

"Let me in, Nella. Let me in! I love you!"

She stood behind the curtains listening, hoping the police would come quickly or she knew he'd get in.

She didn't hear from Eric Clover after that. With a kind

of mechanical numbness she organised Hunt's funeral. She'd almost lost track of her sorrows and what they were.

The funeral passed quietly. She had no feeling of Hunt being there, or with her, as she'd had with her father. People came to the church who had never been near him in the hospital. They came, Eleanor felt, for her mother's sake. Everybody once knew who Huntly Quinton was and now practically nobody did. The vicar called him by the wrong name at one point in the service. "Hunt Quilter bore his suffering with fortitude," he said.

Everybody asked where Hugo was and Eleanor replied, as she always had, that he had a lot on. She hadn't the slightest idea where he was and she felt like telling them so, once and for all.

"You look bloody awful," Marian remarked sympathetically. "I don't think my little brother takes nearly enough care of you. I'm going to tell him so."

Hugo arrived unheralded with Bad Dog three days later.

Eleanor came back from lunch with Peter and Marian to find him in the house. He was sitting reading the paper with Mungo purring on his knee. Already the sitting room had a sort of scattered air as if he'd brought real life with him. He'd made poached egg for lunch. The plate was on the floor and a cigarette stub was floating in his coffee cup. She had the strange sensation of feeling part of the neighbourhood again because he was there too.

"What have you done to your hair?" he said.

"Hunt's dead, you know."

"I know. That's why I'm here."

"Well, you've missed the fucking funeral."

"I'm sorry. I really am extremely sorry, darling. Anyway, I've come to take you back."

"Oh, I can't come back now."

"How soon can you be ready?"

"I'm looking after the cat."

"We'll take Mungo with us of course. He's stayed before. He loves it, and Bad Dog enjoys having him."

"Maybe we can go tomorrow," she said, too fragile to have an argument. "I'll see." He mustn't go without her. "Stay here."

"I can't stay, Nella. I've got to get back."

There was such an aching at the back of her throat. She took his cup into the kitchen but she couldn't see to put it down.

Hugo took it from her. "There was nothing for Hunt. You said that yourself. Don't cry for him."

She started to run the hot water for the washing up. "No."

But the game was over with Eric Clover. Was it a game? Even as the worst waves of loss engulfed her, she never thought it was love.

Hours later the house was straight. In a state of utter exhaustion they had supper and climbed into the car with the animals. At two o'clock in the morning they were only just joining the M1 after Birmingham. Eleanor's head kept falling forward. She slept and jolted awake as Hugo chatted.

"Mr Sharkey died, by the way. The place was in a terrible mess. Police were there, forensic experts and so forth. They stayed for about three days, guarding the house and searching for clues. They thought it was murder."

"Poor old Mr Sharkey."

"Incredible, isn't it. He'd lived there for years in that house, paying the council nothing. No furniture in there of course but the fire going night and day. There was a thousand quid lying about in notes and it turns out he owned a house in Bromley. I had a hair-raising time with that Day woman when I tried to get in to remove his fireplace. I had to use a crowbar."

Eleanor felt for a magnesia tablet.

"I got Edgar Binnie to act as a decoy. He absolutely loathes her. He worked with her at Joy's once. Apparently after the birth of the anti-Christ, she used to sit at her desk in the personnel department with a metal pump strapped to her breast. She tried to persuade her colleagues to take her milk in their coffee."

"But what if they see the fireplace in our house?"

"I'd no sooner got it into the house than Mr Majid appeared. I was aghast. I raced him past the sitting room and up the stairs to the attic to show him where Dave smashed up the skylight. I couldn't think how to keep him there while I removed the fireplace so I drew his attention to a new escape trunk I'd just been using and he was most intrigued. I shut him in it while I hurtled downstairs."

"I hope he was smiling like a badger."

"Yes, he was extremely pleased with that trick. I think he'll invite me to do a spot at the Christmas party in the Town Hall."

The lights of Luton spread out beside the motorway. They were nearly home. In the end, Eleanor thought, putting a hand into the back to cosset Bad Dog, habit makes a haven. At a certain age there can't be any more surprises.

"So you were right about Eric Clover," she said, to get it over.

"It was fortunate you found that ticket."

"I wonder what it meant."

He gave a little impatient shake. "It meant everything. I was about to do one of my usual little courier missions.

We had somebody out there doing a one-off job for us and we expected trouble from an Islamic fringe group. We wanted a magical departure before there was any."

Suddenly, Eleanor grasped everything. "You hid him in one of the trunks?"

"Right," Hugo nodded, as if relieved she knew. "It went superbly. One of my best operations. We'd set it all up with this Turkish magician, Dr Gurbuz and his Death Rays. He was performing in Ankara."

"*Dr Gurbuz?*"

"Dr Gurbuz is a marvellous act. He invites volunteers on to the stage and shuts them inside coffins. They disappear and skeletons pop out instead. It's a huge spectacle with drums and blackness and spotlights. Our man was in the audience, being tailed of course. He went up, got in the coffin and vanished. It worked like a dream."

"What about Eric Clover though?" she said, watching Hugo's long slender hands on the wheel.

"Hmmm . . ." he said, as if hesitating whether to tell her. "Poor old Clover. I wonder if he was just a private investigator. I think it may have been just another job for him."

"Well, what happened?"

"Oh . . . our man couldn't risk it. He shot him."

Silently, in the dark, the tears poured down Eleanor's face and soaked into her skirt. She was crying for Eric, and for Uncle Hunt. She was crying for herself because even the past can change as we look back from further on.

Hugo felt her shaking and put out his hand for hers. "In these games, you know, people tend to get hurt."

As they turned into Holloway Road, Eleanor spoke again. "Who's Our Man?"

"Robin Stewart White," Hugo said.